Paul was evading her questions

But Sierra just couldn't figure out why. She'd steeled herself for a swaggering braggart who would try to impress her with tales of his mountaineering exploits. Instead, she'd met a disarming, slightly goofy regular guy who seemed reluctant to talk about climbing mountains at all.

He was also decidedly better-looking than the man in the blurry Internet photo she'd located. Not too tall, with short, spiky brown hair and brown eyes and the great legs she'd expect from a climber. He had a smile that would stop any female in her tracks—but if he thought he could use that smile to distract her from her purpose here, he'd be disappointed.

She, of all people, was immune to the charms of a mountain climber.

Dear Reader,

The closest I've come to mountain climbing is hiking a few of Colorado's fourteeners—peaks that rise over fourteen thousand feet above sea level. Getting to the top was a major rush—a little taste of what I imagine real alpinists feel.

Overcoming any big obstacle can feel that way—scary, exhausting and triumphant. Some obstacles in our lives can certainly seem as insurmountable as any mountain: a serious illness or the pangs of hurt suffered in childhood.

In *Her Mountain Man* I wanted to write about two people who confront personal obstacles in different ways. Sierra thinks she's conquered the hurts of her past by ignoring them, while Paul feels compelled to face down his personal demons over and over. Neither of them is getting anywhere until falling in love forces them to take a different approach.

I hope you'll enjoy Paul and Sierra's story. Write and let me know. I love to hear from readers. You can e-mail me at Cindi@CindiMyers.com, or write in care of Harlequin Enterprises, 225 Duncan Mill Rd; Don Mills, Ontario M3B 3K9, Canada.

Cindi Myers

Her Mountain Man
Cindi Myers

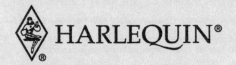

HARLEQUIN®

TORONTO • NEW YORK • LONDON
AMSTERDAM • PARIS • SYDNEY • HAMBURG
STOCKHOLM • ATHENS • TOKYO • MILAN • MADRID
PRAGUE • WARSAW • BUDAPEST • AUCKLAND

Recycling programs
for this product may
not exist in your area.

ISBN-13: 978-0-373-71643-2

HER MOUNTAIN MAN

Copyright © 2010 by Cynthia Myers.

www.eHarlequin.com

Printed in U.S.A.

ABOUT THE AUTHOR

Cindi Myers fell in love with the mountains of Colorado the first time she saw them, and she fell in love with her husband almost as quickly. They met on a blind date and were engaged six weeks later. It's no wonder she writes about romance and people who were meant to be together.

Books by Cindi Myers

HARLEQUIN SUPERROMANCE
1498—A SOLDIER COMES HOME
1530—A MAN TO RELY ON
1548—CHILD'S PLAY
1612—THE FATHER FOR HER SON

HARLEQUIN AMERICAN ROMANCE
1182—MARRIAGE ON HER MIND
1199—THE RIGHT MR. WRONG
1259—THE MAN MOST LIKELY
1268—THE DADDY AUDITION

HARLEQUIN NEXT
MY BACKWARDS LIFE
THE BIRDMAN'S DAUGHTER

HARLEQUIN ANTHOLOGY
A WEDDING IN PARIS
  "Picture Perfect"

HARLEQUIN SIGNATURE SELECT
LEARNING CURVES
BOOTCAMP
  "Flirting With an Old Flame"

CHAPTER ONE

ONLY THE DEAREST OF friends could have persuaded Sierra Winston to risk life and limb—and some very expensive shoe leather—on this wild-goose chase. She looked down at her nearly new pair of Christian Louboutins sinking slowly into the muddy streets of Ouray, Colorado. "Mark, you *sooo* owe me," she muttered, as she pulled one foot, then the other, out of the mud and took stock of her new surroundings.

The Victorian-era storefronts along Ouray's main street looked straight out of a postcard, but the backdrop for this slice of small-town Colorado drew the eye and made Sierra's breath catch in her throat. Snowcapped mountains soared above the former mining town, their icy granite spires and sun-washed slopes making the village and the people in it seem tiny in comparison.

Sierra felt a little sick to her stomach, staring up at those mountains. They reminded her of too many things she'd avoided thinking about for too many years.

That was part of the reason she was here today,

she reminded herself. She would have to face her past if she ever wanted to let go of it, and this was the place to do it.

She started across the street, slowing to allow an open-topped Jeep to pass. The two male occupants of the vehicle whooped and waved at her. She managed a thin smile, conscious of how out of place her designer miniskirt and red stilettos were in a town where most of the women wore jeans and hiking boots. *You're definitely not in Manhattan anymore,* she reminded herself as she reached the opposite side of the street. Here, a life-size bronze sculpture of a bugling elk confronted her.

"Can I help you, miss?" An older man with a thick head of graying hair approached her.

"I'm looking for Sixth Avenue." None of these dirt roads was what she'd term an avenue, but that was the address she'd been given.

"Who's the lucky person you're going to see?" The question was delivered in a jovial tone, but the old man's eyes sharpened. In Manhattan she'd have blown off the question, but this was a small town, where everyone knew everyone else. There was little chance she'd keep her destination secret for long.

"I'm going to see Paul Teasdale," she said.

The man's friendly manner quickly became guarded. "Are you some kind of reporter?" he asked.

Apparently she wasn't the first journalist to have found her way to this remote outpost. Then again, it wasn't every day that the body of one of the most celebrated mountaineers of the twentieth century was recovered from the side of an Alaskan peak by one of the mountaineering stars of the twenty-first century—a man who just happened to live in Ouray, Colorado. Sierra offered her most disarming smile. "It's all right," she said. "Mr. Teasdale is expecting me."

"You want to head two blocks up that way," the man said, pointing. "Though I can't say if he's home right now."

He'd better be home, she thought, *after I flew two thousand miles and drove another forty to see him.* And all because an old boyfriend had asked her to do him this one big favor.

She thanked the old man and set off once more. After hours on a plane and in the small rental car, she'd decided to stretch her legs by walking to Paul Teasdale's house. She walked everywhere in Manhattan, and two blocks didn't seem that far. Sierra had looked forward to a pleasant stroll around town—not an endurance march. The sidewalk ended after only a few yards and she found herself picking her way along another dirt street, this one ascending sharply uphill. Her progress was slow, since she had to stop every few feet to catch her breath in the thin air. This gave her plenty of time to think about what she would say to Paul Teasdale when they met—and how she'd ended up here in the first place.

"I need a reporter for an assignment," Mark had

said the morning he'd called Sierra in her office at *Cherché* magazine, one of the top women's magazines in the country. Mark worked two floors up at the male-oriented *Great Outdoors.*

"Why are you calling me?" As she talked, she searched in her desk drawer for a nail file. "I already have a job. And I don't have time to freelance."

"I already okayed this with your boss. You can work on this assignment and still draw your salary from *Cherché.*"

"What kind of assignment?" Her beat was gossip, glamour and women's issues. *Great Outdoors* specialized in testosterone, grit and gear.

"It's a human interest story. Right up your alley. Top pay and all expenses."

"There has to be a catch."

"Yeah, that's where the favor comes in. This is the kind of story that could make my career—and you're the only one who can write it for me."

She gave up her search for the file and resisted the urge to gnaw the ragged nail instead. The uneasy quaking in her stomach increased with each word from Mark. "What's the story?"

"I've landed an interview with Paul Teasdale. But he'll only talk to you."

Paul Teasdale—a name she'd heard far too often these past few days. "No."

"I know it's a lot to ask," Mark continued, as if he hadn't heard her refusal. "But Teasdale isn't talking to anyone. Rumor is he's angling for a big book contract. My editor already struck out trying to get a story from him, so I took a big chance and offered him you."

"What am I, the sacrificial virgin?"

"You're Victor Winston's daughter."

As if that wasn't a sacrifice of a different kind. Sierra had refused to think of her father for years, and then Paul Teasdale had carried his body down from a mountain and for the past week she hadn't been able to turn on the television or pass a newsstand without seeing or hearing his name. The headlines screamed at her in stark black letters: Famed Mountain Climber's Body Discovered Twelve Years After His Death! Or Twelve Years On Mount McKinley—Body Of America's Most Famous Climber Recovered.

Dead more than a decade, Victor Winston was still a celebrity. No doubt, he would have loved all the attention. Other mountaineers may have been more technically proficient, but no one was better than Victor at playing to the press. Even freezing to death in a blizzard at nineteen thousand feet, he'd radioed details to all the major wire services.

Never mind Sierra and her mother, sitting at home glued to the television and waiting for news. By then, it had been years since fourteen-year-old Sierra had felt close to her father, but the memories of those times were still fresh—days when public acclaim and the allure of summiting the next peak hadn't meant more to him than spending time with his family. In those last few anxious days of his life, she'd listened to the increasingly desperate dispatches from Mount McKinley, hoping for some sign that he was thinking of her, but it never came.

When the transmissions ceased and it was assumed Victor Winston had died, what little love she'd had left for him had died, too. She'd followed her mother's example, presenting a stoic face at the public memorial service after he was declared legally dead, boxing away the pain like old clothes that didn't fit anymore.

Now Mark was asking her to take out those old garments and try them on again.

"I know it's a lot to ask," he said again quietly. "But it's the big break I've been waiting for."

Promotions at Davis Partners Publishing were tough to come by, especially on the testosterone side of the company. The editors of the hot rod, hunting, fishing and other male-targeted publications tended to stay on the job until they suffered heart attacks at their desks. The only way for an assistant like Mark to score a better position was to do something earth-shaking.

An exclusive from Paul Teasdale probably qualified. Mark was one of Sierra's dearest friends, but could she do this, even for him? "What would I have to do?" she asked. Maybe a phone call or two wouldn't be so bad...

"He lives in some little town in Colorado—Ouray.

We'd fly you out there and you'd hang out for a few days, get an idea of what he's like. And I want your personal touch on the story—emotions, opinions, whatever comes to mind."

In other words, he was asking her to bare her soul.

"I'd have to go there and meet him?" She'd avoided looking at any pictures of Teasdale, but she knew what he'd be like—wiry and ruggedly handsome.

It was enough to make her gag.

"Come on, Sierra. Aren't you a little bit curious?" Mark asked. "Don't you think this would help you, too?"

She stiffened. "Help me how?"

"I don't know—answer some questions about your dad. Bring you some closure."

"I don't need any closure, Mark."

"Right. Of course you don't. So interviewing this guy should be no big deal. Think of it as a free vacation to the mountains."

She knew Mark; he wasn't going to let this go. She took a deep breath. "All right. I'll go out there and talk to him. But not only do you owe me that big fat paycheck, when I get home I want dinner at Jean-Georges." The exclusive Central Park restaurant was a favorite of well-heeled foodies.

"Dinner, with champagne and all the chocolate you can eat. And thank you! I'll send down the travel documents as soon as they're ready."

So here she was in Ouray, Colorado, hiking uphill

in high heels and fighting a queasiness in her stomach that had nothing to do with the altitude. She'd lied to Mark when she told him she wasn't curious about her father. She didn't have any questions about how he died—the details had been played over and over in the news the past few days. But since he and her mother had separated when Sierra was ten, she did want to fill in the blanks of his life between then and when he'd died four years later.

What had driven him to risk his life in such hazardous conditions, to spend months away from home and family and suffer all manner of hardships?

What had he found in the mountains that he couldn't find with his wife and child?

Why had he played the part of the devoted father for the first ten years of her life then left her, taking with him a piece of her heart she'd never been able to get back?

Those questions had been enough to override her better judgment and persuade her to leave Manhattan for the wilds of middle-of-nowhere Colorado. She hoped that in talking to Paul Teasdale she could somehow solve the mystery of her father and discover what had driven him to the mountains—and away from her.

PAUL TEASDALE SAW the woman long before she spotted him. He'd climbed onto the roof of his duplex to replace some damaged shingles and had scarcely driven the first nail when he glanced down the hill and

saw a vision in short skirt and crazy high heels dog-
gedly hiking toward him. She stopped every half block
to catch her breath, giving him the opportunity to
study her. Her brown, shoulder-length hair, her narrow
black skirt and crisp white blouse, though simple,
screamed designer pedigree.

He let his gaze linger on her long, shapely legs.
That's what high heels did for a woman.

What was a woman like her doing in Ouray, Colorado, a long way from fancy gyms and designer boutiques? She didn't look like the typical tourist, so that
left the other category of visitors the town had seen
too much of lately: reporters.

Frowning, Paul turned his gaze from the woman
and fished another nail from the pouch at his waist.
He'd really hoped the news media had tired of him and
his refusals to talk to them. Yes, finding the body of
Victor Winston had been an historical moment, but
also an intensely personal one.

Like much of the rest of the country, Paul had been
glued to his television twelve years before, when the
mountaineer had been trapped on Mount McKinley,
the weather keeping his rescuers at bay, infrequent
radio transmissions relaying his plight. Only sixteen
at the time, Paul had vowed to replicate Winston's
historic climb one day.

He'd never dreamed he'd come face-to-face with
his idol upon doing so. He was still processing every-

thing the discovery meant, and didn't care to share his feelings with reporters.

Excited barking from his dog, Indy, announced a visitor. "Hello! Excuse me! Hello!" called a feminine voice.

Paul swiveled ninety degrees and looked down on the woman. She tilted her head toward him, cheeks flushed pink, hazel eyes sparkling. He clamped one hand on the ridgeline to steady himself. "Uh, hi," he stammered. So much for impressing her with his charm and savoir faire.

His golden retriever, Indy, scampered around her, tail wagging. She absently patted the dog. "Excuse me, I'm looking for Paul Teasdale. I was told he lived on this street."

"Are you a reporter?" he asked. Who else would be looking for him these days?

"I am." The woman's expression sharpened and she studied him with a new intensity. "He's supposed to be expecting me. In fact, my visit here was his idea."

Paul blinked, the vague memory of a telephone conversation he'd had last week—one of many telephone conversations last week—sharpening. "What's your name?" he asked.

"Sierra Winston."

This sophisticated beauty was the daughter of the great outdoorsman, Victor Winston—a man who had bragged about never wearing a suit, and who was known in his youth as "potato face"?

Paul almost fell off the roof in his haste to scramble over to where he'd anchored his climbing ropes. He slid down the side of the house and landed directly in front of Sierra. He wiped his hand on his cargo shorts, then offered it to her. "It's a pleasure to meet you, Ms. Winston. I'm Paul Teasdale."

She didn't take his hand. "A moment ago you didn't seem so sure about that."

"Sorry about that. Reporters have been hounding me. I've been doing my best to avoid them."

Her expression relaxed and she took his hand. "I know what you mean. I've gotten a lot of calls from the press lately, too."

He winced. What a clod he was, complaining about his own notoriety, when she'd had her grief and pain made public again after twelve years, all thanks to him.

"You'll be safe here," he said. "I think most of the press have given up and gone home." Indy sat at his feet and leaned against him. "This is Indy, by the way. I promise he's harmless."

A hint of a smile appeared on her lips, then vanished. She reached into her purse and pulled out a mini tape recorder. "Why don't we go inside and start our interview," she said, her tone brisk.

He pictured the chaos that was his living room—climbing gear competed for space with dirty clothes, half-chewed dog toys and cross-country skis he was in the middle of waxing. "Hold on a minute," he said. "Did you just get into town? Where are you staying?"

"I'm at the Western Hotel. And yes, I just got here—my flight out of Denver was delayed."

"I hate it when that happens," he said. "But it's a beautiful drive from the airport, isn't it? What kind of rental did you get?"

"Some little car. I'm not sure what kind. I don't own a car, so I never pay attention."

"Yeah, well, we thought the subway would be finished by now, but they ran into a vein of gold while they were blasting the tunnel and decided to mine that instead of building track."

She stared at him, as if debating his sanity. Usually women laughed at his jokes; maybe his brand of humor didn't play well east of the Mississippi. "Why don't we just get on with the interview?" she asked.

"My house isn't really in any kind of shape for company," he said. "I'll just stow my climbing gear and we can go over to the Western Saloon for a drink," he said. "How long are you staying?"

"My return ticket is for next Monday." She didn't sound very happy about that.

"Then we've got a week. Plenty of time."

He began to roll up the rope, carabiners and harness. "Why don't you use a ladder, like everyone else?" she asked.

"Because I don't own a ladder. Besides, this is more of a challenge." He stashed the gear in a box on the front porch. "Let me get my keys and I'll drive you back to the hotel." He glanced at her feet. "I can't believe you walked over in those shoes."

"I like to walk." But she didn't protest when he returned with his keys and motioned for her to follow him to the red Jeep Wrangler parked beside the house. Indy hopped into his customary place in the backseat, tail wagging.

"There are a lot of great trails around here," he said as he backed the vehicle into the street. "But you might want to think about a pair of hiking boots. They wouldn't go with your outfit, but they'd be a lot more comfortable."

She ignored the remark and pointed to the dog. "Does she go everywhere with you?"

"He. Indy, after Indiana Jones. And yeah, he pretty much goes everywhere with me when I'm in town. When I'm on an expedition my neighbor keeps him for me. Do you have any pets?"

"No."

"Not even a cat?"

"No."

"I thought all single women in the city had cats or little dogs—like they came with the apartment."

She laughed. "No." Then sobering. "I had a cat once. Oliver. He got sick and died."

"I'm sorry. That's tough."

"Yeah."

"So you never got another one?"

"No. It was just too hard."

They stopped at the end of the street. A pickup truck rumbled past on Main, the driver sounding three toots on his horn and waving. Paul returned the greeting. They passed two more pickups and another Jeep between his house and the Western Hotel and Saloon. Every driver slowed and waved, grinning at Paul.

"You have a lot of friends here," she observed.

"I do, but they couldn't care less about me today. They're interested in you." He parked at the curb and climbed out of the Jeep, motioning for Indy to stay. With a sigh, the dog lay down on the backseat.

"In me?" Sierra asked.

"Yeah. They want to know who you are, where you're from, if you're single and what are the chances they could score a date with you."

"You're putting me on."

He held open the door for her. "An attractive young woman always draws attention in a small town where males outnumber females," he said.

Every time Paul stepped into the Western Saloon he half expected to see John Wayne bellied up to the carved-oak bar. The tin ceiling, scuffed wood floors and brass spittoons looked straight off a movie set, but Paul knew they were the real deal.

"Are there really more men than women in this town?" Sierra asked as he guided her toward a booth at the back.

"Have been ever since it was founded by miners in the 1800s. Like those guys there." He nodded to a black-and-white photograph of a group of solemn-faced men with elaborate moustaches that hung over the booth. "They came here planning to get rich and go home, but a lot of them ended up staying. There are a lot more women here now, but even more single guys. They come for the climbing and hiking and skiing and Jeeping and the outdoor lifestyle."

"You don't think women like those things?" she asked.

"Not as many, I guess." He thought of her high heels and miniskirt. "You don't strike me as the out-doorsy type."

"Not really, no."

The waitress, Kelly, sauntered over. "Hey, Paul." She rested one hand on the back of his chair and smiled warmly. "What can I get you?"

"I'll have a Fat Tire. What would you like, Sierra?"

"I'll have a glass of water, thank you." She arranged the small tape recorder, two pens and her notebook on the table in front of her.

He eyed the tools of her trade warily. Right after his discovery of Victor Winston's body he'd been eager to talk to the one person who might understand the mixture of grief, admiration and frustration the find had kindled in him. He'd imagined Victor's only child would understand his admiration for her father and that she'd be able to tell Paul things about his idol he'd always wanted to know. But Sierra was nothing like he'd expected.

He'd tried to find information about her online, but other than her byline on a few articles, he hadn't discovered much. He'd imagined a tomboyish, outdoorsy type—a female version of the young Victor Winston.

Confronted with this beautiful, sophisticated, coolly businesslike woman, he realized how delusional he'd been. Why should this woman want to commiserate with him, much less share intimate details about her life with her father?

She switched on the tape recorder. "Tell me about Paul Teasdale," she said. "I did a bit of research on the Internet, but I'd like to hear your story in your own words."

He shifted in his chair. This was why he didn't do interviews—he hated talking about himself. "What exactly do you want to know?" he asked.

"What led you to become a mountaineer?"

"I enjoy the challenge of climbing, and the sense of discovery. Mountains are one of the last frontiers left to us, remote and largely untouched by development." He climbed places where he was likely the first man to ever set foot, and felt awed and humbled by the experience.

"You say you enjoy the challenge—so is it an adrenaline thing? You get a charge out of the risk?"

He frowned. "That makes me sound reckless. I'm not. My goal is always to climb safely."

"Safety is a relative term at nineteen thousand feet."

"Things have changed since your father's day," he said. "We have more high-tech gear now, though I prefer to climb without supplemental oxygen as much as possible." He watched as she made note of this. "How technical do you want me to get here?" he asked. "I can bore you with descriptions of safety harnesses, if that's what you really want to know."

She looked up from her notes, hazel eyes meeting his, her expression troubled. "What I really want to know is what would lead a man to repeatedly risk his life on the side of a mountain?"

The question was less an accusation than a plea. Paul searched for some way to answer her. "Climbing mountains is only part of any climber's life," he said. "A big part, but the climbers I know aren't irresponsible about it, whether it's their job or their avocation." He rearranged the salt and pepper, as if lining up his defenses against her probing looks and questions. "I don't look at it as abandoning my responsibilities," he said. "I mean, I don't really have any."

"So you're single. No significant other?"

He shook his head. He hadn't exactly avoided serious relationships, but his schedule—away half the year or more—made attachments difficult.

"What about your parents? Don't they worry about you?"

"My parents have been my biggest fans. They're very happy for me." He paused while Kelly put down their drinks. Ordinarily he would have encouraged her to stay and chat, but Sierra didn't seem to want to linger on niceties.

Her question about his parents fueled his curiosity, and he leaped at the opportunity to turn the conversation momentarily away from him. "What about you? Tell me about growing up with Victor Winston," he said. "What was it like having such a legend for a dad? Did he share his love of mountains with you?"

It was her turn to look uncomfortable. "I'm supposed to be interviewing you, not the other way around," she said.

"Yes, but the whole reason I agreed to this interview was to get a chance to meet you." He leaned across the table. "Your dad was my hero when I was a kid. I was fascinated by the incredible things he did. He wasn't content to follow in other climbers' footsteps. He insisted on finding new routes up some of the most challenging peaks. And he was one of the first to create high-quality films of his expeditions, so that others could share the experience. I wore out a tape of a British documentary made about him. You know the one—about his ascent of K2?"

He grinned, remembering a point in the film where others in Victor's climbing party wanted to turn back in the face of adverse conditions. Victor had insisted on forging on, and stood at last at the summit, a solitary conqueror, wind whipping back the hood of his parka, the huge grin on his homely face saying all that needed to be said about his triumph. Paul had watched that part over and over, imagining himself in Victor's boots, victorious after overcoming insurmountable odds.

She shook her head. "I don't think I ever saw that one."

"Aww, you gotta find a copy. You're even in it."

"I am?" She looked surprised.

"Well, you were probably too young to remember, but there's this great shot of him carrying you in a sling on a training climb." Amazing to think that the woman before him was that baby. "He said he wanted you to learn to climb almost as soon as you could walk."

Her expression softened. She looked...almost wistful. "I don't remember that. How old was I?"

"Two? Maybe a little older. I'm not good at judging ages. How old are you now?"

"Twenty-six."

"The documentary was made in 1986, so you would have been two."

"And you were four. How old were you when you saw the film?"

"Ten. It wasn't released in the U.S. until 1992, after Victor became more well-known." Before she could ask *why* he'd been watching the film—a subject he didn't care to discuss—he shifted the conversation again. "Are you hungry? I forgot to eat lunch and I'm starved. I bet you didn't get a chance to eat, either."

"I had a pack of pretzels on the plane."

"I've gotten to where I pack a lunch when I fly. You

never know when you'll get a chance for real food. Do you care if we order a pizza?"

"Uh, I guess not."

He signaled Kelly and ordered a pepperoni-and-mushroom pizza, and another beer for him and more water for Sierra. He really was hungry, but mostly he was glad of the chance to shift the conversation away from his least-favorite topic—the dark circumstances that had driven him to climb mountains for a living.

CHAPTER TWO

SIERRA KNEW PAUL was evading her questions; she just couldn't figure out why. She'd steeled herself for a swaggering braggart who would try to impress her with tales of his mountaineering exploits. Instead she'd met a disarming, slightly goofy, regular guy who seemed reluctant to talk about climbing mountains at all.

He was also decidedly better-looking than the blurry Internet photo she'd found had indicated. Not too tall, with short, spiky brown hair and brown eyes, and the great legs she'd expect from a climber. He had a smile that would stop any female in her tracks—but if he thought he could use that smile to distract her from her purpose here, he'd be disappointed. She, of all people, was immune to the charms of a mountain climber.

"Why don't we get back to the interview," she said when they were alone again.

His brown eyes were wide and innocent. "I figured you'd be sick of listening to me talk by now."

"You keep changing the subject." She tapped her

pen against the pad of questions. "Tell me more about yourself."

He threw one arm across the back of the booth and looked out over the saloon. Was the pensive profile an act, or was he really that uncomfortable with her? "I don't know why you want to know all that stuff about me," he said. "The real story is your father and all he did. I'm only a small part of it, the person who found his body. I thought you came to talk about that."

She never liked to talk about her father, yet he was, in truth, the reason she was here. Because the magazine wanted this story from the point of view of Victor Winston's daughter. And because she was determined to uncover some insight that would help her reconcile the father she'd adored as a child with the man who'd abandoned her when she was older. In some ways, Paul seemed to know Victor Winston better than she had; could he be the key to reconciling her two views of her father?

"I need to know your background in order to give readers a complete picture," she said. She consulted her notebook. "I read that the first mountain you climbed was Long's Peak, here in Colorado. Why did you pick that one?"

He faced forward again. "Because I was living in Boulder at the time and it was close. Say, did you and your mom ever go with your father on his climbs?" he asked. "I know you didn't climb with him, but were you at base camp? Or waiting in a nearby village?"

"No. We never accompanied him on his climbs." The idea of her pampered, patrician mother in some frozen base camp was preposterous. "I'm sure he would have thought we were in the way."

Even as she said the words, a memory flashed in her mind of her at six or seven, weeping and clinging to her father as he prepared to leave on an expedition, begging to go with him. Victor had knelt and embraced her. "Maybe I'll take you with me someday, sweetheart," he'd said. "When you're a little older. We'll go climbing together."

She blinked rapidly, and sipped water to force down the knot in her throat. She hadn't thought of that memory in years.

"Base camps are like little villages, you know," Paul said. "There are all kinds of people there— men and women, and some children, too. There's a fourteen-year-old boy who's already summited four of the seven sisters. His parents climb with him."

"Not my idea of fun family bonding," she said. Though if her father had asked her to follow him into the icy, forbidding wilderness that was a high mountain peak, there had been a time when she would have gladly done so.

The waitress, Kelly, delivered plates and silverware. "Pizza will be out shortly," she said.

"Great." Paul rubbed his hands together in anticipation. "I'm starved. I remember reading about your dad waiting at base camp for two weeks for conditions to clear enough to climb Everest," he said. "He lived off oatmeal and peanut butter for the rest of the expedition." *He made a face.* "I hate oatmeal."

"But you became a mountain climber despite the hardships. Why?" This was a question she would have asked her father; the one her readers would surely want to know.

"It's hard to explain."

"Try."

He hesitated, then said, "There's a tremendous sense of accomplishment in climbing. The freedom of setting your own pace. The challenge of testing yourself."

"That describes how climbing makes you *feel,* but is that the only reason you do it—for the adrenaline rush?"

"You don't think that's enough?" The grin was a little more lopsided now, a little less sure.

"Most people don't spend their lives looking for a rush," she said. "Is that really all you get out of mountaineering?"

"Let's put it this way—why did you become a reporter?"

"You're trying to shift the conversation away from the interview again."

"No, no, this relates, I promise. You're asking me to explain what I do for a living. I want to hear your reasons. Did you always have a burning desire to write? Or did you just fall into the job after college?"

"I always wanted to write," she said. She'd majored in journalism and had gone to New York after she'd graduated, determined to get a job at a magazine. She'd never even thought about a different job.

He nodded. "I guess mountaineering is like that for me. It feels like what I was meant to do."

"Climbing mountains? Come on—that isn't a real job. It doesn't offer a service or entertainment or improve the world. And unless things have changed since my father's day, the pay is pretty lousy." Her mother had had the money in the family; in darker moments, Sierra had wondered if that was the chief reason her parents had wed.

"He made money selling the film rights to his expeditions, didn't he?" Paul said. "He was one of the first climbers to do that. Today, it's all about sponsorships. I have a couple of mountaineering-equipment manufacturers and outdoor-clothing suppliers who sponsor me. And I've got an agent who's trying to get me to go on the lecture circuit."

"My dad did some of that, too. There was nothing he liked better than a captive audience."

"Really?" He leaned forward, eyes alight with interest. "Was he like that at home, too?"

The man was good, but she'd dealt with tougher interview subjects. She focused once more on her notebook, reserve firmly back in place. "You still haven't answered my question. Why do you climb mountains?"

"There are some people who think that each person fulfilling his or her potential is enough of a reason to do anything," he said.

"Let me guess—you picked that up from a Sherpa you met on Everest."

"I met him on Nanga Parbat, actually. Do you like your job? Do you enjoy what you do?"

"Most of the time, yes."

"I enjoy mine, too." He leaned back to allow room for Kelly to set down the pizza.

"What is there to enjoy about risking frostbite and hypoxia on some lonely mountain peak? About living on peanut butter and oatmeal for days in the middle of a blizzard?"

"All those things you mentioned—the frostbite and danger and lousy food—that part of mountaineering sucks," he said. "But the climbing itself—pitting myself against the elements and then reaching my goal—in those moments, I feel so incredibly alive. I think it's the closest any human can get to immortality."

She stared at him. "Aren't you a little young to be worried about immortality?"

He dragged a slice of pizza onto his plate and refused to meet her gaze. "High mountains are one of the few places still relatively untouched by human development. The scenery is spectacular, like nothing you'll find on the flatlands. Your father must have felt the same way. Didn't he ever talk about it?"

"No." She laid her pen aside and helped herself to the pizza.

"Then I don't really know how to explain it to you. Tomorrow, let's go up into the mountains so you can see for yourself."

"What do you mean?"

"We'll take a Jeep tour. Go up above tree line. It'll give you a whole new perspective on what I do and why I do it."

Would it? Or was this just another way for him to avoid answering her probing questions? "And if I refuse?"

"You want to get a good story, right? I'm better at showing what I do and why than sitting here talking about it. If we were up in the mountains, I think I could explain things better."

She could see his point. Putting a subject in an environment where he felt comfortable could sometimes get him to reveal a side of himself she might not otherwise see. "If I go with you, you'll answer my questions?"

"I'll do my best." He offered another charming smile. "Hey, you came here to work, but it doesn't mean you can't have fun, too."

"Barreling up a mountain in a Jeep isn't really my idea of fun."

"Then you don't know what you're missing. Better skip the skirt and heels," he said. "And wear a coat. It gets cold up there."

"Anything else I should bring?"

"No, I'll take care of the rest."

"Just come prepared to talk."

AN HOUR LATER, with blisters the size of half-dollars on both heels and heartburn from the delicious but too-spicy pizza, Sierra climbed the stairs from the Western Saloon to the hotel overhead. Unlike her tiny, contemporary apartment, the accommodations were spacious and furnished with an old-fashioned brass bed and a wooden chest of drawers, table and chairs that looked straight out of the 1800s. Chintz curtains and a matching comforter added to the visit-to-Grandma's feel. It was a nice enough room, but she wasn't sure she wanted to spend a whole week here.

When she'd found out Mark had booked her for seven days and six nights here in the back of beyond she'd been livid, but since she'd only picked up the tickets this morning, it had been too late to do anything about it. Did he really think it would take her a week to do this interview?

Granted, Paul wasn't exactly spilling his guts into her tape recorder, but she'd find a way around his reluctance to tell his story. And as soon as she wrapped up the interview she'd be heading to the airport to change her flight, no matter what it cost.

She kicked off her shoes and lay back in the bed, trying to organize her whirling thoughts. The interview with Paul hadn't gone quite as she'd hoped, but she'd gotten some material she could use. Tomorrow she'd dig deeper; she was nothing if not stubborn. She could already feel the story taking shape: a portrait of two mountain climbers—the laid-back boy wonder versus her single-minded father.

A knock on the door roused her. She shoved off the bed and went to look through the peephole. The waitress from the saloon downstairs stood frowning up at the door, arms crossed, foot tapping impatiently.

Sierra released the chain and opened the door. "Can I help you?" she asked.

"Hi. I'm Kelly. From the Saloon?"

Sierra nodded. "I remember."

"I'm on break and thought maybe we could talk."

"About what?"

"Oh, you know. The town. Fashion. New York. I overheard Paul say you were from there."

Was it a passing mention, or had the waitress been eavesdropping? Sierra had planned on interviewing some of the locals about their notorious neighbor, so she might as well start with this young woman. Maybe Kelly could provide some interesting background on what Paul was like when he wasn't scaling mountains. Sierra held the door open wider. "Come on in."

Sierra guessed Kelly was about twenty-one or twenty-two. Dressed in low-slung jeans and a black polo shirt with the Saloon's logo, she might have been mistaken for any small-town waitress. But her jeans were an expensive name brand, and her pointed-toe boots had a three-inch heel and a designer pedigree. Her hair was cut in the latest style. She might be waitressing in an out-of-the-way restaurant, but she clearly wanted to set herself apart. "Have a seat," Sierra said, indicating the room's only chair, and settling herself on the side of the bed. "My name's Sierra, by the way. Sierra Winston." She waited for the last name to ring a bell, but Kelly gave no indication that it registered, which made Sierra relax a little more. She'd had enough of competing with her father's ghost for one morning.

Kelly sat in the chair and crossed her legs, jiggling one foot. "Are you a reporter or something?" she asked.

"Yes. I'm a writer for a magazine called *The Great Outdoors.*"

"So you and Paul just met?"

"That's right."

The foot stopped jiggling. "I was wondering. He didn't exactly act like you were strangers. He was being really friendly."

"He isn't usually friendly?" The idea didn't jive with the Paul she'd seen so far.

"Not with reporters." She laughed. "The other day a couple approached him while he was eating lunch in the Saloon and he threatened to sic his dog on them. As if Indy would hurt a flea! But the reporters didn't know that, I guess. They backed off."

"He agreed to an exclusive interview with my magazine," Sierra explained. "It was all arranged before I flew out here. So, what can I do for you?"

"What part of New York are you from?"

"I live in Manhattan."

"So you're right where all the action is. Do you see many Broadway shows?"

"A few."

"Know any actors or actresses?"

"Not well, but I've met a few. One of my neighbors is an actress, I think."

"No kidding. What's her name?"

Sierra shook her head. "I don't know." She didn't know most of her neighbors' names. "People in the city like their privacy."

"I guess so. I mean, she probably doesn't want to be bothered by fans and everything."

"Right." Sierra doubted her neighbor was famous enough to be recognized by anyone on the street, much less mobbed by fans.

"You're so lucky," Kelly said. "New York has everything—the theater, night life and great shopping. Those are killer shoes, by the way." She nodded to the heels that lay on the rug beside the bed. "Totally impractical here, but they look awesome."

"Thanks. But you're right—they're useless on these dirt streets. I'm supposed to go on a Jeep tour into the mountains tomorrow and I guess I need to find some hiking boots to wear."

"What size are you? About an eight?"

"Yes."

"I've got a new pair I've hardly even worn. I could lend them to you." Her gaze settled on the heels once more. "And maybe you'd let me borrow those? I have a hot date tomorrow night."

The heels were brand-new and had cost more than the week's accommodation at the hotel. But Sierra needed the hiking boots by tomorrow and Ouray didn't look as if it boasted a lot of shoe stores. Besides, she liked Kelly, who so clearly craved more excitement than this small town could offer. "It's a deal," she said.

"Great." Visibly more relaxed now, Kelly settled back in her chair. "I'd like to live in Manhattan one day. What I really want to do is act, but I guess there are probably plenty of waitressing jobs there."

The longing in the younger woman's voice struck a familiar chord in Sierra. She'd arrived in Manhattan with one thousand dollars in her bank account, clips from her college newspaper and a determination not to leave until she landed a job. She badgered every publisher in Manhattan until she found work as a copy editor at one house and a receptionist at another. She'd shared a tiny apartment with three other women and had worked practically around the clock for the first year. But eventually she'd landed a writing job and a few years later had moved into her own apartment. So who was to say Kelly wouldn't make it as an actress, as well? "I think it's almost a requirement that aspiring actors and actresses have waitressing jobs on the side," she said. "Do you have any experience—acting, that is?"

"Only with local community theater. But I'm saving my money and I'm going to go there and take my chances soon."

"When you're ready to move, I can give you the names of some places to look for an apartment and roommates, and some casting agencies who might be able to help you," she said. She'd interviewed several people at top agencies for a story for *Cherché* only last year.

"That would be great." Kelly looked around the room. "So what do you think of Ouray? It's a lot different from the city, isn't it?"

"It might as well be on another planet," Sierra admitted. "But the scenery is breathtaking."

"The people are nice, too," Kelly said. "Of course, being a small town, everyone pretty much knows everybody's business, which makes it hard to have much privacy, if you know what I mean."

"Then give me the scoop on Paul. What's he like?" If Paul was so reluctant to talk about himself, maybe Sierra could gain some insight from those around him.

"Oh, he's a lot of fun. Very…" Kelly tilted her head, as if searching for the right words. "Thoughtful. Considerate. I mean, some guys only think about themselves. Some women, too, I guess. But Paul is really interested in other people's opinions. We went out a few times and he always wanted to know what I thought about the movie, or my views on local politics. Little stuff like that."

"So you dated." Her fingers itched for her notebook to write some of this down, but she didn't want to risk interrupting the flow of conversation. She could make notes later.

"Only for a little while. Paul's not interested in set-tling down and neither are most of the women he's dated. I know I wasn't. Besides, how can you have a relationship with a man who's gone half the year climbing mountains?"

Right. One of the many problems in her parents' marriage. "Why do *you* think he climbs mountains?"

"Don't those guys always say they climb because the mountain's there?" Kelly shook her head. "Seri-ously, I have no idea. He says it's something he loves to do. It doesn't seem any crazier than a lot of things guys around here do. In the winter, this hotel is full of men, and a few women, who come here just to climb the ice in the ice park. Then you have the Jeepers and hikers in the summer, and the skiers and snowmobilers in the winter. There are folks whose whole lives revolve around their sport. I guess they're dedicated to it the way I'm dedicated to acting."

The way Sierra was dedicated to writing? No, it wasn't the same at all. Writing hadn't taken over her life, and it didn't separate her from her friends and family the way climbing did. "Does he have any family nearby?" she asked.

"I don't think so. His parents live in Texas—Dallas, maybe? I think he came here to be close to the mountains."

Of course. No matter what other positive traits he might possess, Paul still had the glaring flaw of loving big piles of rock more than anything else.

Kelly stood. "I have to get back to work. I get off late, so I'll leave the boots for you at the front desk."

"Thanks." Sierra retrieved the heels from the rug. "Take good care of them," she cautioned as she handed them over.

"I'll treat them like gold." Kelly paused in the doorway. "When you see Paul tomorrow, ask him to tell you about his secret swimming hole in the mountains. It'd make a great story for your article."

"Thanks, I'll do that."

When she was alone again, Sierra sat on the side of the bed and contemplated her bare feet. The Louboutins were the most expensive shoes she owned, and her favorites. Paul had better give her one heck of a story to prove he was worthy of such a sacrifice.

PAUL MET SIERRA AT EIGHT the next morning in the Western Hotel lobby. She attracted plenty of attention as she strode across the lobby, dressed in slim-fitting jeans and a sweater that emphasized her curves. Her long hair was plaited in a single braid that hung down her back, and she carried a leather jacket. Paul stood a little straighter, pleased that he was the one she was coming to meet, even if she was only doing so in hopes of completing their interview.

Maybe things would go better between them today. He hadn't done a very good job of explaining himself yesterday. Part of it was his own fault—he'd thought talking to Victor Winston's daughter would somehow be different from an interview with any of the other journalists who wanted his life's story served up neatly on a platter. Today, he hoped he and Sierra could find a middle ground. He was prepared to talk about finding Victor's body, and he hoped that she could help him know the real man behind the famous mountain climber's public image.

"You look all ready to go," he said when she stopped in front of him.

"I am. I even have boots." She held out one foot for him to admire.

"I was wondering if you'd brought any with you. You probably don't have much call for them in Manhattan."

"I don't. I borrowed these from Kelly."

"From Kelly?" Sierra had been so focused on grilling him yesterday he was surprised she even remembered the waitress.

"Actually, I traded my heels for her boots—temporarily."

Had there been some silent communication between the two women he hadn't picked up on? "When did all this happen?"

"After you left last night. She and I had a long talk." Her smile was closer to a smirk. "She told me all about you."

He tried to think of any embarrassing stories Kelly might have shared with Sierra. Unfortunately the list was long. He could be absentminded when he was planning an expedition, and more than once he'd forgotten about a date they'd arranged, or she'd had to pay for a meal because he'd accidentally left his wallet at home. He always paid her back, but still—those stories didn't make him look good.

They'd dated off and on for a couple of months, but his long absences had gradually cooled their ardor. Last he'd heard, she was seeing a real-estate tycoon from Telluride.

"I've got everything we need in my Jeep, so let's go." A few minutes later, they were headed out of town. Indy sat in the backseat, ears flapping in the breeze.

"You really did mean it when you said the dog goes everywhere with you," Sierra said.

"Yep. You never know when a dog will come in handy." And as much as he usually enjoyed his own company, it was good to have someone to come home to after a long trip.

"An interesting philosophy," she said, writing in her notebook.

"Are you going to write down everything I say today?" he asked.

"That's sort of the idea behind an interview." She looked amused.

"I was hoping we could get to know each other a little first. Off-the-record."

She studied him a moment. "Do I make you uncomfortable?"

"I don't like talking about myself."

"But you agreed to this interview. From what I understand, it was your idea."

So much for his brilliant ideas. "I thought talking to Victor's daughter might be easier than talking to someone who had no connection to the story." He glanced at her. "And I figured I owed you."

"Owed me?"

"It's my fault you're having to go through your father's death all over again, after twelve years."

"You don't owe me anything," she said. "But if it'll make you more comfortable, I'll save most of my questions for later. I'm happy to spend the morning gathering a little background."

The background stuff was exactly what he didn't want to talk about, but he'd humor her. "You're allowed to have fun while you work," he said. "Tourists come here and pay big money for the kind of tour I'm giving you today."

A smile flirted with her lips. "I'll remember that."

Just outside of Ouray, the highway began to climb

up a series of switchbacks. Through the trees, they glimpsed steep valleys and soaring peaks. "You don't get views like this in Manhattan," Paul said.

"No." Gripping the seat with both hands, she glanced at the drop-off on her right side. Approximately three feet from the Jeep's tires, the pavement fell away to nothing. "Aren't you taking these curves a little fast?" she asked.

"Don't worry. I could drive this stretch of highway blindfolded. It's really only dangerous in winter. This time of year it's a lot of fun."

"What's fun about taking chances?" She peered at the drop-off again. "Just because you're familiar with a situation doesn't make it less dangerous."

"But you can't let a little risk keep you from doing what you want to do." He downshifted to take a steeper grade. "I don't take foolish chances, but I want to really live." Having come face-to-face with death made him value life all the more. Every time he made it back from that precipice safely, he was more aware of every heartbeat and every breath.

"I think a person can live a very fulfilling life without ever risking death," she said.

"Some people probably can," he said. "Guess I'm not one of them."

Near the top of Red Mountain Pass, he turned the Jeep off the highway onto a narrow gravel road that wound uphill through stands of aspen already beginning to turn gold. Even in August the air up here hinted at fall, the breeze cool on Paul's bare skin. He breathed deeply the aroma of purple asters that bloomed in profusion along the road.

"This road once led to the old Tomboy Mine," he explained. "It was used to transport ore into Telluride."

"So mountains aren't the only things that interest you," she said. "You know the history of the area, too."

"History is interesting," he said. "It's everywhere you look around here. So many reminders of the past are out in the open—old buildings, mine trams, ore carts. People walked away from some of the old settlements and mines over a hundred years ago and left everything behind. Stuff survives a long time in the thin mountain air."

They passed the remains of mining buildings, the wood weathered to silver-gray, orange-yellow mine tailings spilling down the hillsides. "Whenever I drive this road, I try to imagine what it must have been like for those miners, with their wagonloads of ore, negotiating these same curves," he said. "They didn't have the benefits of four-wheel drive and power brakes."

"They must have been pretty desperate to make a living, to work such a dangerous job in such remote and wild surroundings."

"I prefer to think of them as brave adventurers who relished the freedom of life on their own terms."

They stopped at a stream crossing and a bull elk

raised his head to watch them. The gurgling of the water sounded over the low rumble of the Jeep's engine. Other than an occasional burst of birdsong and Indy's enthusiastic panting from the backseat, there was no other sound. "We haven't seen any other cars in a while now," Sierra said.

"Traffic's pretty light today. Come back Saturday and you'll see bumper-to-bumper Jeeps sometimes. Four-wheel-drive clubs from all over the world come here to run these trails."

"I guess a lot of people like to get back to nature in a powerful, gas-guzzling machine."

He laughed. "I knew there was a sense of humor somewhere under that veneer of cool sophistication."

"Are you saying I'm a snob?"

"You have snob potential, but I don't think you really are." A woman who'd trade her fancy high heels for a waitress's hiking boots could never be called a snob.

"I can't decide if that's an insult or a compliment."

"Not an insult, I promise." He pulled the Jeep into a turnout on the side of the road. "There's a trail here that leads back to some neat old mine buildings and a waterfall. Let's check it out." He collected his pack from the back of the Jeep, whistled to Indy and led the way up a narrow trail through the trees.

"How long have you lived in Ouray?" she asked, walking close behind him while the dog bounded ahead.

"About five years. I'd been coming here for a few years to climb the ice in the winters. I decided I wanted to live at altitude, near good climbing to help me stay in condition."

"So Ouray was a practical choice."

"That, and I really like it here." He held a low branch up out of her way until she'd passed. "It's beautiful. Not too big. The weather's nice—what's not to like?"

"Maybe the fact that it's three hundred miles from a major city? Almost a hundred miles to a mall?"

He laughed. "If I want to buy anything, I order it off the Internet."

"Spoken like someone who doesn't understand the allure of shopping."

"Guilty as charged."

The trail began to climb and they fell silent as they scrambled up the incline. Indy took off in halfhearted pursuit of a squirrel, then circled back to Paul's side. Sierra fell farther and farther behind, until Paul stopped to wait for her. "Want me to get behind and push?" he called.

She glared at him. "Some of us…are used to… breathing air…that contains…oxygen."

"More like smog for you. Stick around a few weeks and you'll get used to the thin air up here."

She caught up with him and stopped to catch her breath. "I've got it figured out now," she said after a moment.

"Got what figured out?"

"Why you're crazy enough to climb mountains. Lack of oxygen has obviously left you brain damaged."

"I never said I wasn't crazy." Their eyes met and he felt the heat of attraction. She had the most amazing eyes, so full of emotions he couldn't read. He'd like to know her well enough to interpret those emotions.

She looked away. "We'd better get going," she said, and moved past him up the trail.

He shrugged. Not that he minded the view from this angle, but he couldn't help but feel she'd moved ahead to get away from him—or from something in herself he made her feel.

CHAPTER THREE

MORE THAN A LACK OF OXYGEN had stolen Sierra's breath back there on the trail—for a moment, when she'd looked into Paul's eyes, she'd wanted him to kiss her. The impulse had surprised her. Yes, he was good-looking and entertaining. His evasiveness of her questions frustrated her and his fascination with her father puzzled her, but he had a zest for life and a goofy wit that disarmed her. When he did answer her questions, she sensed that his replies were honest, and he had none of the arrogance she'd expected from a star in a sport that demanded supreme self-confidence.

She'd awakened this morning prepared to endure the day's activities for the sake of the story, but she was actually having a good time, thanks to Paul. Maybe it was their surroundings that influenced her feelings toward him. Odd, how such vast open spaces could seem so intimate. She and Paul were truly alone, without another soul around.

The important thing was to not let her attraction to Paul get in the way of writing a good story. Her job was to find out everything she could about him and his motivation for climbing, and share that with her readers. If she also gained some insight into her father, that would be a bonus.

If she could only understand why her father had been so determined to conquer mountains while he avoided any obstacle at home, maybe she could find a way to reconcile her feelings for him—to mingle love and hate into acceptance.

"The mine ruins I was telling you about are just ahead." Paul touched her elbow, pulling her from her reverie. "On the left."

She stopped and studied a square black hole in the side of a hill, framed by leaning timbers and blocked by a rusty metal grate. "What was the name of the mine?" she asked.

"I don't know. There are dozens of them scattered around these mountains. Maybe hundreds."

"I wonder how many of them ever made any money?"

"Apparently a lot of them—for a while, anyway. There are still people with mining claims up here, still looking to strike it rich, I guess."

They continued on the trail, which began to slope down, making the hike easier. "I'd forgotten there are still places this remote in the United States," she said.

"I guess there's not much hiking in New York City," he said.

"There are trails in Central Park, though I haven't explored them. When I was a girl, I used to go hiking with my dad." She hadn't thought about those trips in years. Climbing this trail—the smell of pine, the crunch of gravel beneath her feet—had brought the memories rushing back.

Those trails had seemed long and steep to her, but her father must have chosen the easiest routes, and modified his long strides to accommodate her short ones. When she tired, he'd carry her on his shoulders; the whole world had looked bigger and brighter from that lofty perch.

"Where did you go?" Paul asked.

"Everywhere. Weekends when he was home, we'd get in the car and drive. We'd pack a lunch and hike for hours. We were living in northern California then, so we had a lot of trails to choose from. We'd stay out all day, just him and me."

"In the Sierra Nevadas, right? You must have been named after them."

She frowned. "Yes. I still can't believe my mother let my father name me after a mountain range."

"At least he didn't saddle you with Shasta or Bernina or Lhotse. Sierra's a really pretty name. Maybe that was his way of bringing together two things he loved most."

She swallowed past a sudden knot in her throat. As a girl, she had looked forward to those hiking trips with her father with all the anticipation of Christmas. The opportunity to have him all to herself for an entire day had been better than any gift she could have received.

"How old were you when you went hiking with him?" Paul asked. His expression was gentle, full of warm interest. The caring in his eyes emboldened her to reveal more than she ordinarily would have to someone she'd known such a short time.

"This was probably between the time I was six or seven and ten. Before my parents split up and Mom and I moved back east to live with her parents."

"I didn't know your father and mother were divorced."

"Technically they weren't. I think my mom hoped her leaving would convince him to stay home more and give up risking his life climbing mountains. She told him he had to choose between his family and the mountains." She watched Paul's face, waiting for his reaction to this statement.

"And he chose mountains," he said matter-of-factly, as if of course this was the only choice. Sierra turned away, disappointment a bitter taste in her mouth.

She'd begun to imagine that because Paul was more laid-back than her father, that because he had room in his life for friends and other interests and even a dog, he might be different from her dad. She'd have to be on her guard not to make such misjudgments again.

This reminded her of the real purpose for this trip. Why not use this glimpse into Paul's real nature to develop her article?

"So you don't have any regrets about the choices you've made?" she asked Paul.

"Regrets? Why should I have regrets?"

"You chose to become a mountaineer instead of going to college and starting a more conventional career. You travel much of the time instead of having a more stable home. You work mostly alone…"

"No regrets," he said firmly. "I'd go nuts if I was imprisoned in a cubicle in an office. And I do have a home—right here. I'm here about half the time. Being away makes me appreciate it that much more."

"And working alone so much of the time doesn't bother you?"

"You don't write with a partner, do you?"

"No, but I still work with other people at the office."

"And I have climbing partners and participate in large expeditions from time to time," he said. "I'm no hermit who hates people. But I like the challenge of facing a mountain alone. Climbing solo requires you to live very much in the moment."

"How very Zen."

"It is. People spend too much time worrying about the future."

Or fretting about the past, she thought. This trip to Ouray was turning into more of an excavation of her history than she'd been prepared for, dredging up memories of her father—both good and bad. She'd anticipated some of that, of course. Her father, or at least his body, was the link between her and Paul. But trying to understand her father's motives by examining Paul's wasn't working out that well. Paul was so much warmer, much less interested in the spotlight than her dad. Yet he clearly felt a strong connection to her father.

That mystery both drew her and frustrated her. The simple story she'd expected to write about two generations of mountain climbers grew more complex by the hour. And Paul grew more intriguing.

The idea unsettled her, the way that moment on the trail when she'd craved his kiss had unsettled her. She didn't want to be attracted to a man who climbed mountains for a living. It didn't matter that he wasn't like her father—he still had that one very big strike against him.

Fine. She wasn't at the mercy of unpredictable emotion. Whatever brief chemistry had passed between she and Paul, it wasn't permanent or fatal. She'd step back into her reporter's shoes and get this story done. And Paul would be just another interview subject—more memorable than most, but not the kind of man who would change her life.

PAUL SENSED THE CHANGE in Sierra's attitude. The easy warmth of her manner vanished, and was replaced by the cool, all-business demeanor she'd greeted him with yesterday. "We should get back to the car now," she said. Not waiting for an answer, she turned and started back the way they'd come.

"Wait," he called. "You haven't seen the waterfall."

"I don't need to see the waterfall."

He hurried after her, Indy at his heels. "Be careful,"

he called. "If you take a wrong turn you might end up at the bottom of a mine shaft."

She said nothing, but slowed down.

"What's wrong?" he asked when he caught up with her.

"Nothing," she said. "I just think we should get back to the Jeep and get on with our interview."

"Wait a minute." He stepped in front of her, forcing her to stop. "Something happened just now and I want to know what it was."

"You're imagining things." She tried to move around him, but he refused to give way.

"We were getting along great, like friends. Now it's almost like you're angry with me."

"I'm not angry with you. I don't even know you."

"The whole point of this outing was for the two of us to get to know each other better. And I thought we were making pretty good progress. Until we started talking about your dad." As soon as he said the words, he felt sick to his stomach with guilt. "I'm sorry," he said. "I've been an idiot."

She looked puzzled. "What do you mean?"

"I've forgotten you're in mourning," he said. "Because of me, you have to relive the pain of your father's death all over again, and here I am, asking you all these questions."

"You don't have anything to feel guilty about," she said calmly. "I mourned my father a long time ago. Long before he died."

She moved past him again, and this time he let her go. He wasn't sure he believed her when she said she didn't mourn Victor. When she'd told Paul about the hikes she and her father had taken when she was a child, he'd heard the sadness in her voice. Maybe she didn't miss the father who'd been away climbing mountains, but some part of her grieved for the man who'd been with her on those childhood hikes.

Paul wished he could have known that man. To him, Victor Winston was the larger-than-life figure who'd inspired him and encouraged him. The movies Victor made of his expeditions had introduced Paul to the mountains and shown him the possibilities of a world far different from the one in which he lived every day. That was the figure whose footsteps he'd set out to trace when he climbed McKinley.

To come upon Victor's body, so small and fragile, light enough to carry down on his back, had been a shock. It reduced Paul's own accomplishments, made them less meaningful. Every time he climbed a mountain, he thought about staring down death, but finding Victor had been a different kind of confrontation with the end. He'd spent years comparing himself with his hero, inspired to live up to Victor's achievements. Now, he had to wonder if he'd end up like the man he'd admired—dying slowly on a mountainside, all alone.

The idea shook him still. Would Victor say it had all been worth it? It was a question Paul had wanted to ask Sierra.

He remembered again the light in her eyes when she'd talked about hiking with her father, having him all to herself.

Maybe it was guilt, or some latent desire to connect with his hero, but Paul felt protective of Sierra. She might be a tough city girl, but he'd glimpsed a vulnerability in her that touched him. These past few hours had changed his feelings about her visit and this interview.

Now, instead of wanting to know Victor better, Paul wanted to know Victor's daughter.

THEY WALKED IN SILENCE back to the parking area. By the time they reached the Jeep, Sierra felt more in control of her emotions. Talking about her father with Paul had been a bad idea. He only saw the inspiring public figure—the man who had charmed millions in his videos and interviews. Paul didn't see the reserved, uncommunicative man who had spent days shut away from his wife and daughter. The man who had made no protest when her mother took her away, and whose visits and calls became more sporadic as the years passed. The more of himself her father gave to the world, the less he had for Sierra.

Paul wouldn't understand any of that, and though his concern for her and her feelings seemed genuine enough, how could it possibly be real? He didn't know her, and she was leaving in a few days anyway.

Being here, surrounded by snowcapped peaks with

a man who had literally walked in her father's footsteps, had obviously shaken her up more than she wanted to admit. Maybe Paul was right and grief was responsible for part of her emotional turmoil. Better that than to imagine Paul himself had breached her usual reserve. She still couldn't believe she'd told him about those hikes with her dad. She'd never told anyone about them—she hadn't even thought of them in years. And yet she'd poured out the story to him with only a little prompting. What was it about him that inspired such confidence?

Back at the Jeep, she settled into the passenger seat, once again determined to turn the conversation back to the interview. Indy took his place on the backseat and Paul started the engine, then turned to her. "Just to warn you, this next section of the road can be a little hairy in places, so hold on tight."

"We aren't going back the way we came?"

"This road goes into Telluride. There's some terrific scenery you don't want to miss. We'll come back along the highway."

"Oh. Okay."

They set off with a lurch, and Sierra steeled herself for a harrowing drive. But after the first couple of miles proved to be not much different from the ground they'd covered so far, she began to relax. Maybe he'd been trying to frighten her—to shake up the city girl. She smiled. If he thought he could scare her off that easily, she'd show him he was sadly mistaken.

She was about to tell him as much when they rounded a sharp curve and she looked out over… nothing.

Or rather, a lot of empty space, below which was a valley painted in green and gold. The ground fell away sharply a scant foot from the side of the Jeep. She held on to her seat belt and bit back a gasp.

Paul seemed oblivious. He steered the Jeep over and around potholes and rocks, whistling under his breath. "What happens if we meet another car?" she asked.

"Uphill traffic has the right of way, so they'd have to back up."

He inched the Jeep around a series of hairpin curves, tires spinning in the gravel. Sierra bit her lip to keep from crying out. No matter what, she refused to let Paul see she was frightened.

Suddenly he slammed on the brakes. The back end of the Jeep skidded sideways in the gravel. Indy let out an excited bark and Sierra yelped. "What's wrong?"

"Look, up there on that rock." Paul pointed to his side of the road, to a pile of rock at the base of the cliff walls. "It's a marmot."

She stared at the fat, furry animal, about the size of a small dog. "You sent us into a skid to point out a marmot?"

"Aww, that wasn't much of a skid. Did you bring a camera with you?"

"Why? Do you want your picture taken with the marmot?"

"That's not a bad idea," he laughed, "but there's probably better scenery around than that."

He grinned, flashing white teeth. In the sun, gold flecks sparkled in his eyes, and a two-day growth of beard gave him the ruggedly handsome look Hollywood stars worked hard to cultivate. Her girlfriends would no doubt agree with her that he qualified as better scenery.

"I didn't bring a camera," she said. "The magazine will be sending a photographer later."

He started the Jeep forward again. They were above tree line now, and the air was considerably cooler. Sierra retrieved her jacket from the backseat and put it on. She decided to avoid looking to the side or down and focus on staring straight ahead. She normally wasn't afraid of heights, but the sheer drop at her side was unnerving.

A carved wooden sign declared their arrival at the top of the pass. Paul parked the Jeep over to the side and they climbed out. "Check out this view," he said, spreading his arms wide. "Isn't it incredible?"

The mountains rose around them, their snowcapped peaks startlingly white against a turquoise-blue sky. Brilliant sun illuminated a kaleidoscope of red rock, golden aspen, dark green fir and rich brown earth. The colors were almost too vivid, the sun too bright. She felt lost in such vastness, like Alice plunged down the rabbit hole—she was in a world where she didn't quite fit, yet fascinated by her surroundings.

"That tallest peak—the one that comes to a sharp point—is Mount Sneffels," Paul said. "You'll see it in ads and on postcards all over the place around here. The wide peak next to it is Wilson Peak. The sort of rounded one is Teakettle Mountain, and that one over there is Gilpin Peak."

"Have you climbed any of them?" she asked.

"I've climbed them all. Most of them aren't technical. *You* could climb them."

"Ha! Not me. If I want to be on top of something tall, I'll ride the elevator to the top of the Empire State Building."

"I know you went hiking with your dad, but did you ever climb with him? I mean, other than that training climb he carried you up when you were a baby."

"I told you, I don't remember that one. And no, I never climbed with him." She stooped and picked up a handful of gravel and began tossing pellets out into the bottomless valley below.

"I figured he would have had you out there with him as soon as you could carry a pack."

"I guess by the time I was old enough, he'd changed his mind." She ignored the ache in her chest. If her father had ever asked her to climb with him, she had no memory of it—she remembered only her longing to be with him, and his silence on the subject. "My mother wouldn't have let me go with him, anyway," she said. "It was dangerous enough for a man, let alone a child."

"These mountains aren't dangerous. Schoolkids around here climb them all the time."

"Next you'll tell me they all know how to kill and skin an elk before their tenth birthday."

"Hey, I'm telling you the truth. Just a few days ago the paper ran pictures of a bunch of fifth-graders on top of Matterhorn Peak. That's that one right there, to the left of Wilson."

She still couldn't tell if he was putting her on or not. If he thought he could tease her, maybe it was time she turned the tables a little. "Is your secret swimming hole anywhere near here?" she asked.

To her amusement, the tips of his ears reddened. "Who told you about that?"

"Kelly said I should ask you about it—that it would make a great story for my article."

"Just wait till I see her again." He turned toward the Jeep. "Come on, let's eat lunch."

"You *have* to tell me the story," she said, following him to the car. "Or I could just ask Kelly."

"I'll tell you, but you have to promise not to use it in your article."

"Aww, come on. It can't be that bad."

"You have to swear," he said.

She held up her right hand, palm out. "I swear. What's the story?"

He leaned into the backseat and pulled out a plastic tote bag. "We'd better eat in the Jeep," he said. "There's really no place else to sit."

Practicing patience, she slid into the passenger seat and accepted the sandwich he handed her.

"Hope you like turkey," he said. "It's on cranberry wheat, from the Timberline Deli. There's chips, too." He fed Indy a potato chip.

"Thanks. So what about the swimming hole?"

"I'll get to that." He unwrapped his own sandwich and arranged it on the console between them, then handed her a bottle of water.

He opened another bottle and took a long drink. "Okay, here's the story. Which—I remind you—you promised to not reveal in your article."

"I promised, I won't. Get on with it."

"A few years back, I went hiking above Red Mountain Pass. It was a hot day, even for the mountains. I was on a trail I'd found on an old map and it showed a spring alongside a creek up there, so I decided to try to find it.

"I passed a bunch of No Trespassing signs, but ignored them. I mean, this was way up, where there weren't any roads. I didn't think anyone possibly lived there."

"So the spring is your private swimming hole?" What was so potentially incriminating about that?

"Not mine. I found it, all right. It wasn't very big, but big enough for one person to soak. I stripped off and slipped in. After that long climb, it felt great. The next thing I know a bullet whizzes over my head and this old guy comes storming out of the trees, cussing and waving his hands around."

"Who was it?"

"Some old guy who'd set up a mining claim. He had an old camper back in there that he'd pulled up with a four-wheel-drive truck."

"And he was the one who'd put up the No Trespassing signs."

"Exactly. He was really bent out of shape about me being there. I tried to apologize and explain, but he wouldn't hear it. He grabbed up my clothes and ordered me out of there."

"He took your clothes?"

"Yeah. I bargained with him to let me keep my boots and my pack, or I might not have made it down, but he wouldn't give back anything else. He told me if I didn't leave in a hurry, he'd shoot me and bury me in an old mine shaft. I didn't know if he was bluffing or not, but I didn't want to take a chance."

"You had to hike out of there *naked?*"

"Yep."

The fact that he was blushing made the story all the more real. She could only imagine the looks he must have gotten, strolling into town wearing only hiking boots and a backpack. "What did you do when you got back to town?" she asked.

"I had a bandanna in my pack and made a kind of loincloth, so I wasn't completely indecent. But of course word got around." He made a face. "Not my best moment."

She tried to hold back the laughter, but it was no

use. The image of him strolling into town in his bandanna loincloth was too priceless.

"Come on," he said. "It isn't that funny."

"It's just so…so not how I pictured you."

"You mean you haven't been fantasizing about me naked? I have to say I'm really disappointed."

She fought down a blush of her own. Okay, so she was physically attracted to this guy. He was good-looking and funny and her hormones had decided to respond to him, but she was too much of a professional to let him know about it. "I had this idea that you'd be this macho he-man, really full of himself," she said.

"Is that the kind of guy you usually hang out with?"

"No. But in my experience, anyone who's fanatical about a sport or a hobby or a job has that kind of personality."

"And you think I'm a fanatic?"

"I think anyone who regularly risks death for the sake of getting to the top of a mountain qualifies as a fanatic."

He gestured out the window, at the panorama in front of them. "Take this view and multiply it to the tenth power," he said. "It's incredible, and once you've experienced it, you want to experience it again and again. Plus, there's this tremendous sense of accomplishment, that you did this really difficult thing, and didn't let the hardships defeat you."

"Are you saying there's nothing down below that compares?"

"Not that I've found yet."

"What about love? People say that's the ultimate high."

"I've never been in love." His eyes met hers. "What do you think? Do you think love is the ultimate high?"

She wanted to turn away, as if looking into his eyes too long would reveal all her secret hopes and fears. Of course, that was ridiculous, so she held his gaze and kept her voice even. "I've never been in love, either," she admitted. "But I hope so. Why else would people go through so much for it? Why have so many songs and stories and works of art been created in homage to it?"

"You could say the same thing about mountains. Maybe that feeling I get when I'm up there is similar to being in love."

"You can't love an inanimate object that way."

"For a woman who says she's never been in love, you sound as if you know a lot about it."

"Only because I know what it should be. What I want it to be." Now it was her turn to try to read his feelings in his eyes. How could he compare the adrenaline rush of physical accomplishment with warm, emotional feelings? "Enjoying doing something, or even that feeling of accomplishment you talked about, isn't the same as love," she said.

"If you say so." He looked away. "I want to make it into Telluride while there's still plenty of time to look around."

Coward, she thought, and bit into her sandwich. Maybe mountain climbing attracted men who weren't capable of sharing their feelings with others. Her father had certainly fallen into that category.

And yet—when he'd been telling her about his embarrassment at the hot springs, Paul hadn't seemed at all arrogant or distant or incapable of love. She'd liked that Paul. The real man, the one she should portray in her article, probably lay somewhere between those two extremes. The mystery, as it had been from the first, was how to persuade that man to show himself, to her and to her readers.

CHAPTER FOUR

THEY MADE IT DOWN the mountain to Telluride, where a tour of Telluride's boutiques, followed by dinner at a three-star restaurant, improved Sierra's mood considerably. Indy had settled down in the backseat of the Jeep while Paul and Sierra explored the town. Despite his admitted preference for the great outdoors, Paul had waited without complaint as Sierra tried on clothes and shoes, and had even offered to carry her packages. If he could be that good a sport after the hard time she'd given him on the mountain, maybe there was hope for the man yet.

"I fulfilled my part of the bargain, spending the day getting to know you," she said as the waiter delivered the Irish coffee she'd ordered in lieu of dessert. "Now we really need to get back to the formal interview."

"We've got plenty of time," he said. "Let's not spoil dinner with a bunch of boring talk about me."

"You're terribly modest for someone who's supposedly one of the best in his field."

"Trying to flatter me into submission?" He hit her with another of his engaging smiles. "I promise I'll tell you everything you want to know," he said. "But let's not spoil tonight. Tell me more about you."

His continued stalling intrigued her. Did he have some secret he was hiding? If so, what was the best way to get him to reveal it? "I filled you in on the basics last night," she said.

"Then let's go beyond the basics. I already know you don't like climbing mountains—what do you like to do? Any hobbies? Do you collect ceramic frogs or take belly-dancing lessons or read Sanskrit in your spare time?"

She laughed. "No, no, and no."

"So what do you like to do? You must have a life outside of your writing."

"I collect netsuke—little Japanese carvings that were designed to attach items to the sash of a man's kimono."

"I know what they are," he said. "I should have guessed."

"Why do you say that?"

"Your father had a fantastic collection."

"He did not! You're making that up."

"I am not. They were donated to the Denver Museum of Nature and Science upon his death. You didn't know?"

She shook her head, confused. Her father had given her her very first netsuke, red coral carved into the shape of a dragon, when she was nine years old. He'd gotten it while in Japan for a winter climb of Mount

Fuji. "It must have been something he picked up after my mother and I moved away."

She couldn't believe she hadn't known this about him. She'd been fourteen when he died, and he'd left everything to her mother. She must have disposed of the netsuke collection—but why hadn't she mentioned it to Sierra?

"How do you know so much about my dad?" she asked Paul. How did he know more than *she* did?

"I already told you that documentary inspired me to want to climb. Dallas isn't exactly a climbing mecca, so I had to learn about the sport from books and movies, like your dad's. I decided that in order to succeed, I should model myself after the top climbers—your dad was one of the best, so I read everything I could about him, to try to learn all his secrets."

"What secrets did you uncover?" She kept her voice light, but she steeled herself for some shocking revelation—another family, a drug habit. After the news about the netsuke, she realized how much of a stranger her father had been.

"Climbing secrets," Paul said. "I unearthed an old interview where he talked about a new route up K2. He never got a chance to climb it, but I did last year."

"You climbed all his routes, didn't you?" she said, remembering her research.

"I still have a few to go."

"That's what you were doing on McKinley—retracing his last climb."

"Right." The waiter brought the bill and Paul took out his wallet. "I know that's what you came here to talk about, and I promise I'll tell you everything," he said. "But can it wait until tomorrow? I'm having a good time tonight, and it's not a pleasant subject."

"All right." For a man who'd been missing, either literally or figuratively, for much of her life, her father still elicited such strong emotions in her. She would never look at her netsuke collection the same way now, wondering if he'd owned a similar piece, or if he'd thought of her when he began his own collection.

"Are you ready to go?" Paul asked.

"Yes." She'd had too much of her father, and maybe too much of Paul, for one day.

They walked in silence to the Jeep, past bars whose open doors spilled music and restaurant patios lit with strings of paper lanterns. Sierra might have been walking through the East Village. She felt a sharp pang of homesickness.

But there was nothing of New York in the drive back to Ouray, the highway a black ribbon winding past blacker countryside, without even the light from a home appearing for miles. The only illumination was from the millions of stars overhead, like glitter scattered with a heavy hand. Sierra shivered and drew her coat more tightly around her. Everything about this place, from the towering mountains to the vast star-strewn sky, seemed designed to emphasize man's insignificance. Some people claimed the big city was impersonal, but she couldn't agree less. This emptiness was far more lonely and demoralizing to her.

Paul parked in front of the hotel and came around to help her out, though that was unnecessary. He took her hand and held it. "Thanks for humoring me and coming with me today," he said. "I had a good time."

"I had a better time than I expected," she said. "And you're right—seeing you in your element, as it were, will add to my article. What time should we meet tomorrow?"

"Look me up whenever you're ready. No rush." He leaned close. She caught the scent of warm male skin—soap, sweat and spice—then felt the caress of his lips, soft on her cheek. "Good night," he murmured, then released her.

"Good night," she mumbled, and hurried blindly into the hotel, her cheek still burning from the kiss.

It had been such an unexpected gesture, so gentle and courtly, even. Her whole body was warmed by it.

Paul definitely had a knack for throwing her off balance. Was it a skill he'd cultivated, or was it something in her that was responding to him in such unexpected ways?

Much as he aggravated her at times, Paul was impossible not to like. She might as well enjoy his company, as long as they had to spend so much time together.

There was nothing wrong with liking him. The trick was not to forget herself and like him too much. It had been a long time since she'd fallen for a man, but she remembered the feeling—the rush of fascination, the sense of danger, the exhilaration even of arguing with him. Paul kindled all these things in her. It was a heady combination, but one she wasn't interested in pursuing. Not now. Not with Paul.

SIERRA WOKE THE NEXT morning to bright sunlight. Why is it, she wondered, that hotel-room curtains always have a gap that focuses the morning sun directly onto the face of anyone trying to sleep in? Was it a required design element, like the television that can't be comfortably viewed from any of the room's furnishings?

Pondering such trivia kept her from thinking about the kiss she'd shared with Paul the night before, though she'd fallen asleep remembering the feel of his lips on her cheek. Did he romance every new woman in town this way, or did she, as a visiting journalist, get special treatment?

The blare of "New York, New York" roused her from her reverie. She grabbed her cell phone and shoved herself into a sitting position. "Hello?"

"Good morning." Mark's voice was entirely too cheerful for seven in the morning. Though of course it was nine in New York. "How are the mountains?"

"The mountains are fine," she said.

"And how's our mountain man? Are you getting a lot of great material for your article?"

"Lots of great stuff." She suffered only a twinge of guilt as she thought of the single page of notes she'd collected. Though she and Paul had spent quite a bit of time together, he'd successfully avoided answering most of her questions. "It's going to be a great story," she said to Mark, with forced cheerfulness.

"You okay?" he asked. "You sound funny."

"It's only seven here. I'm still in bed."

"Oh." He cleared his throat. "I'm not, um, interrupting anything, am I?"

"Mark!"

"Sorry. I mean, it's none of my business."

"I came here to work, not to pick up men."

"Forget I mentioned it. I know you're not like that. I just…listen, you're okay with this, right?"

"Okay with what?" She rubbed her right temple, fighting the beginning of a headache.

"I mean, dredging up the past isn't too painful for you, is it?"

"No, of course not." Before leaving New York, she would have said her father was a part of her past she'd dealt with long ago. But being here with Paul, unearthing memories of her dad—both pleasant and not so pleasant—made her realize the pain she'd locked away was still there.

"It isn't the easiest subject in the world for me," she admitted. "But I think you were right. I needed to come here and hear Paul's story, for closure." When she left Ouray, maybe she'd have a more complete picture of Victor Winston, and a glimmer of understanding about what drove him.

"I started feeling guilty as soon as you left," Mark said. "I really do appreciate this."

"I'll make sure you show that appreciation when I get home. Speaking of which, what was the big idea of exiling me to this place for a whole week? Do you really think it's going to take me that long to do an interview?"

"I thought you could use the time off."

"Seven days?"

"You're entitled to four days bereavement leave for the death of a parent. I thought you might like to use it."

"Mark, that was way out of line."

"I know, I'm sorry. I told you I felt guilty about all this. But I hear Ouray's beautiful—take some time off and enjoy yourself."

"I'm coming home as soon as I've gotten all the information I need."

"Be that way, then. I really do appreciate you taking the assignment. The publisher saw me in the elevator yesterday and he congratulated me on landing this story. Before last week, I don't think he even knew my name."

"That's great. I'm happy to hear it. Don't worry about me, I'll be fine."

"I'm counting on you to turn in a killer story. It's going to be the lead for the November issue, did I tell you?"

"No, you didn't." A shiver of excitement swept through her at the idea of a cover story—followed closely by apprehension. She'd have to work harder to pin down Paul and get him to tell her his whole story—not just what had happened on McKinley, but all that had led to that moment.

"If you need anything from this end, research or anything, let me know," Mark said.

"I will." They said goodbye and she slid her phone shut and stared through the gap in the curtains at the snowcapped mountains. Most people probably saw tremendous beauty or awe-inspiring majesty when they looked at those peaks. Sierra remembered her mother helping pack her father's climbing gear as he prepared to leave on yet another expedition. Tears streamed down her mother's face as she worked, and her father pretended not to notice.

Once, when eight-year-old Sierra had begged her father to stay home, he'd patted her shoulder and smiled. "This is what Daddy has to do," he'd said, as if he was a coal miner who was forced to risk death to feed his family.

But what was it about mountain climbing that he "had" to do? As she'd grown older, Sierra had decided her father used climbing to avoid his other responsibilities, including taking care of his family. After all, who could be expected to remember to change the oil in the car or renew the insurance policy when there was an expedition to Everest to plan?

Was Paul as irresponsible? He'd mentioned being so involved in his work he'd stood up Kelly on dates. Maybe he wasn't really a "new breed" of climber at all—just the same fanatic in different clothes.

The idea focused her determination. No more wasting time with Paul Teasdale. She was going to pin him down and make him answer her questions. Then she'd write a story the readers of *Great Outdoors* would never forget.

She was putting the finishing touches on her makeup when someone knocked on her door. Had Paul come looking for her?

Her visitor wasn't Paul, but Kelly, red high heels in hand. "Thanks for the loan," Kelly said, handing over the shoes. "They were a big hit."

"I'm glad to hear it." Sierra glanced from the glamorous shoes in her hand to the hiking boots on her feet. "I guess I should buy some boots of my own."

"Just borrow those for the week." Kelly gave the boots a dismissive wave. "I have others." She sat on the edge of the unmade bed. "How'd it go with Paul yesterday?" she asked.

The chance to discuss the situation with another woman, especially one who knew Paul, was too good to pass up. Sierra set the shoes on the dresser and pulled up a chair across from Kelly. "Yesterday was interesting," she said. "I'm supposed to be interviewing Paul, but he doesn't talk much about himself."

"Yeah. Unusual in a guy, right?"

"Right. So, how long have you known him?"

"Since he moved to town five years ago."

"And you know him pretty well?"

"I can tell you he has a pretty nasty scar on his chest."

"Oh?" Sierra grabbed her notebook and jotted this down. "Was he injured in a climbing accident?"

"I don't know. Like you said, he doesn't talk much about himself."

"What about his family? Do they get along? Does he have brothers and sisters?"

Kelly frowned. "Are you asking me to dish dirt on my friend?"

"No!" Sierra set aside the notebook. "I'm simply trying to get some background on him."

Kelly relaxed a little. "I'm sorry. I really can't help you, though—I don't know anything."

"And I'm sorry if you thought I was out of line. I promise, I'm not writing a negative piece. It's just helpful to have input from other people who know the subject of a profile like this, especially if the subject is as modest as Paul." And as closemouthed.

"If I think of anything interesting, I'll let you know," Kelly said.

"Thanks for the tip about the private swimming hole story."

"You asked him?"

"I did!" Sierra laughed. "Though he made me promise not to use the story in my article. Did you see him when he hiked back into town?"

"Oh, yeah. People lined the streets to get a look. We could have sold tickets."

"He seemed to be a pretty good sport about it."

"That's Paul. He never gets too worked up about anything."

Sierra thought of his patience while she shopped yesterday, and his calm as he navigated the steep, winding road. Was he really so Zen—or merely emotionally detached? What would it take to set him off? "Have you ever seen him lose his temper?" she asked.

Kelly shook her head. "Never. He's just not that type of guy."

Levelheadedness was certainly a good quality, but weren't there times when being more emotional was appropriate? How could a man who professed to be so passionate about mountains be so even-keeled about the rest of his life?

Sierra was aware of Kelly studying her. Did she think Sierra was a little *too* interested in Paul? Time to change the subject. "How was your date?" she asked.

"Oh, it was great." Kelly crossed, then uncrossed her legs, her expression somber. "Were you serious the other day, when you said you could put me in touch with some people in New York who could help me?"

"Absolutely."

"My boyfriend is talking about paying my way, so I might be moving out there sooner than I thought."

"Generous boyfriend," Sierra said.

"Yeah, he really is."

"Let me know when you're ready and I'll give you a list of names and numbers," she said.

"Thanks." Kelly stood. "And thanks again for the shoes." She grinned. "You should have seen my boyfriend's eyes pop when I walked in wearing them."

"Thank you for the boots. I'd probably be crippled now without them." Sierra followed Kelly to the door. "Have you seen Paul this morning?" she asked.

"No. He's probably still repairing his roof. If he's not at his house, you might try the hot springs. Or he could be hiking one of the trails around town."

"All right. Where is the hot springs?"

"Just as you come into town, on the right side of the highway. But this early in the day, he probably won't be in the pool. He goes there to climb."

"To climb? At the hot-springs pool?"

"There's a rock wall that's popular with local climbers. They can climb in the morning, and hit the pool in the afternoon."

Of course. Some people drank coffee to get going in the morning, Paul climbed rock cliffs. He was one of that breed of men who seem to think something isn't worth doing unless it's difficult, painful and carries the risk of serious injury or death.

Her mother had once said that if she could have figured out a way to make it more dangerous, she wouldn't have had to nag her father about mowing the lawn. Apparently Paul had found a way to make even a relaxing trip to hot springs risky.

SOME PEOPLE RELAXED by doing yoga or jogging. Paul preferred climbing. Scaling a wall of rock or ice forced him to focus on precisely where to place his hands and feet and when to shift his weight. When he was climbing, there wasn't a lot of room in his head for other things.

But this morning, even climbing couldn't keep out thoughts of a certain shapely journalist who pretended to be cool and aloof, but who had shown signs yesterday of unexpected warmth. After she'd left him last night, Paul had wondered if he should have kissed her lips instead of her cheek. The thought of how she might have reacted had kept him awake for hours.

His climbing partner today, Josh Merton, didn't help keep Paul's mind off Sierra. "What's the story with you and that hot brunette?" he asked, as he and Paul prepared to set anchors for a new route up the pool wall.

"She's a reporter interviewing me for a magazine article," Paul said.

"I thought you didn't talk to reporters."

"She's not just any reporter."

Josh laughed. "I can see that. I guess for a woman who looked like that I might sacrifice my principles, too."

"It's not like that." Paul stepped onto a jutting

chunk of rock and found a handhold in a crevice overhead. He began to climb.

"Don't make the route too tough," Josh said. "Remember, this is for kids. Some of them have been pretty sick, I guess, so the idea is to challenge them, but not freak them out." Josh had volunteered to help with several groups of kids from The Children's Hospital in Denver who were participating in four-day vacations in the San Juan Mountains sponsored by the local Elks Lodge.

"Right." Paul looked up the slope, studying his options.

"You ought to come help with the climb," Josh said. "There's supposed to be seven kids and their families participating. We could always use more volunteers."

"No, thanks," Paul said. Josh was the kind of guy who was at ease with anyone and everyone, but Paul wasn't so comfortable around crowds of strangers, especially a bunch of critically ill children and their families. He wouldn't know what to say to them, and he didn't think he'd be able to hide his emotions.

"Will you be too busy romancing your reporter friend to help me out?" Josh persisted, beginning a route parallel to Paul's.

"She's only here until Monday," Paul said. "And I'm talking to her because she's Victor Winston's daughter."

"Oh." A shower of gravel bouncing down the slope

emphasized the single syllable as Josh scrambled for a new foothold. "That's heavy."

"Yeah." When he'd agreed to talk with Sierra, he hadn't thought much about the potential emotional impact of such a meeting. He'd been focused on the chance to learn more about his childhood hero—the chance to, in a way, bring the man whose body he'd hauled down the side of a mountain back to life.

"So, is she glad you found her dad, or upset that you brought the whole story back into the open after so many years?" Josh asked. He stopped a little above Paul on the wall, flattened against the rock and looked back at his friend.

"She hasn't said." Paul hammered an anchor into the wall. Though she'd relaxed a little around him yesterday, Sierra had been careful not to reveal too much of herself.

He'd enjoyed hearing about her childhood with Victor, but when he'd pressed for more, she'd cut him off. Was it because her parents separated when she was so young?

The idea that his hero had abandoned his wife and daughter bothered Paul. Wouldn't Sierra have seen her dad on weekends and summer visits? Yet she hadn't known about Victor's netsuke collection. Paul wondered if it would be possible to find out when Victor had begun collecting. Had the gift to his daughter sparked his interest? If so, why hadn't he shared that interest with his only child?

The more time he spent with Sierra, the more questions he had. And he couldn't say all his questions concerned her father. The woman herself drew him. He couldn't remember when he'd enjoyed being with someone more. And that one kiss…

"Are you going to lean there against the rock all morning, or are you going to climb?"

He looked up and saw Josh several yards above him. Silently cursing his inability to concentrate, he quickly hauled himself up beside his friend.

They made it to the top of the wall without further comment, setting anchors along the way, then hurried back down. Indy greeted them enthusiastically as they dropped to the ground, barking and licking Paul's face. "Good boy," Paul said, rubbing the dog's ears.

The two men rested a moment against the sun-warmed rock, enjoying the view of the hot-springs pool a short distance away. A few swimmers did laps in the lanes on one side of the steaming pool, while a trio of small children took turns on the water slide. The familiar sights made Paul feel more at home here than any place he'd lived since leaving his parents' place for Everest the summer after he'd graduated from high school. Until he'd decided to move to Ouray, he'd drifted from place to place. Ouray was the first community where he'd felt like putting down roots.

"Speaking of hot chicks, I saw Kelly at Smuggler's

last night." Josh returned to his favorite subject—women.

Paul began gathering his climbing gear. "Was she with that real-estate guy?"

"I don't know. She was on her way back from the ladies' room when we passed in the hall. Then I lost her in the crowd."

"She was probably with him. Keith somebody or other. She seems really into him."

"She told you that?"

"Sure. Why not?"

Josh shook his head. "How is it you stay friends with all the women you used to date? All my ex-girlfriends would just as soon cut out my liver and feed it to their dog."

"That's because you let things get serious and then you break it off. They end up angry and hurt. The women I date are friends. I never let things get too deep. We have a good time, but keep it light."

"Yeah. And why is that?"

"Why is what?" Paul took off his climbing helmet and added it to the pile of gear.

"Why are you only out for a good time? Don't you want to find someone to be with long-term?"

Long-term? A word that meant commitment, even permanence. "I don't live the kind of lifestyle that's compatible with relationships," he said. "My future's too uncertain."

"Everyone's future is uncertain," Josh said. "As for

your lifestyle—mountain climbing didn't stop Victor Winston from having a family."

Paul remembered the hurt in Sierra's expression when she'd talked about her father. "Maybe all that will happen for me later," he said. "Right now I'm too busy to settle down."

The two friends carried their gear to Paul's Jeep. "Where's your next expedition?" Josh asked.

"I'm not sure. I'm considering climbing in Nepal next summer."

"So you'll be here for ice season." In winter, a portion of the Uncompahgre Gorge at the south end of town was transformed into walls of thick ice, which drew professional and amateur climbers from around the world.

"Maybe," Paul said. "I've been invited to join a team that's climbing Fitz Roy Mountain in Argentina this winter. I haven't decided yet."

"You ought to stick around," Josh said. "A lot of female climbers show up for the Chicks with Picks events. You might meet somebody who wouldn't freak out about the whole mountain-climbing thing."

There were a few professional women climbers who might understand the attraction of peak-bagging. He knew of at least one couple who climbed together, though the thought made Paul shudder. Having someone he loved climbing with him would be too much of a distraction. Worrying about her safety would be too stressful, the possibility of seeing her suffer too painful.

He shoved the last of the gear into the Jeep and closed the tailgate. "I don't know about dating a woman climber," he said. "I couldn't impress her with my exploits. And if she was a better climber than I am, I don't know if my fragile ego could handle it."

"I'll have to be sure to mention that if that reporter decides to interview me."

"Sierra? Why would she interview you?"

"For background on you. All the dirt and gossip."

"What dirt and gossip?"

"I'd have to make something up," Josh said. "It would be worth it to get to know her better."

"Forget it." He called Indy and ordered the dog into the Jeep, ignoring the flare of anger at his friend. Was it the idle threat of rumors, or Josh's interest in Sierra that upset him so?

"The Railbenders are playing at The Outlaw tonight," Josh said. "You going to be there?"

"I might."

"I'll save you a spot at my table—at least until I find a good-looking woman to fill it. You could bring Sierra with you."

Would she agree to come to The Outlaw with him? Could he somehow convince her that doing so was necessary for her story? But how pathetic was he if that was the only way he could get a date? "I don't know if Sierra would be interested," he said.

"Isn't that her, headed our way? You can ask her."

Paul whipped his head around and saw Sierra, hair

blowing across her face as she trudged up the road toward them. He was out of the Jeep, going to meet her, before he even realized what he was doing. He had that crazy vertigo feeling again, as if the world had tilted.

Sierra was red-faced and out of breath by the time Paul reached her. "You should have called and I'd have come to your hotel and picked you up," he said, taking her arm and escorting her the last few yards to his Jeep.

She didn't resist, and even leaned on him a little. "I like to walk," she said when they stopped.

At the vehicle, Indy greeted her with a happy bark and much waving of his plumed tail. Josh stepped forward, hand extended. "Hello," he said. "I'm Josh."

"Sierra Winston, meet Josh Merton," Paul said as the two shook hands. "Don't believe half of what he tells you, especially if it's about me."

"Why is that?" Sierra asked.

"Don't listen to him," Josh said, still grinning. "He's fallen and landed on his head a few too many times. It's made him paranoid."

"I'm only trying to protect her from you," Paul fired back. "The local women don't buy your ladies' man act anymore."

"He's just jealous because I won the best legs competition at Rotary Park last year." Josh winked at Sierra. "He only got honorable mention."

"Only because I'd spent the summer in the Himalayas," Paul said. "I was a little pale."

"A little pale? The judges had to wear sunglasses to keep from being blinded by the glare."

Sierra laughed. "You should take your act on the road," she said. "It's very entertaining."

"We were a big hit in Katmandu," Josh said. "Though they didn't get all our jokes in Tanzania."

"The two of you have climbed together?" Sierra asked.

"A few times," Paul said.

"We climbed Everest together," Josh said. "It was the trip of a lifetime, but now I prefer to stick to the local fourteeners or scaling the ice here in the winter."

"Fourteeners?" she asked.

"Colorado has fifty-four peaks over fourteen thousand feet in elevation," Josh explained. "Fourteeners for short. I leave the bigger stuff to this guy here." He clapped a hand on Paul's shoulder.

Paul shrugged off Josh's hand. "What can I do for you?" he asked Sierra.

"We need to sit down together and continue our interview," she said.

"Right." He'd promised to talk to her today. What would she think of him when he spilled his story? And how much of it was he willing to tell her? He could talk about climbing and about Victor, but there were some parts of his personal life he never mentioned to anyone. Call it superstition, but not talking about bad memories was his way of keeping them safely behind locked doors. If he wanted to rehash his past, he'd see a therapist, not a reporter.

"I thought we could conduct the interview at your house," Sierra said. "I want to see where you live."

At least he'd cleaned up the place since that first day. "It's nothing special," he said. "But you're welcome to see it." Conducting the interview at his house wasn't a bad idea. If the conversation got too personal, he could always show her pictures or souvenirs from his expeditions. He'd play the part of the reckless mountaineer—that was what magazines wanted, wasn't it?

If she asked what drove him, he'd keep his answers vague. If George Mallory could announce that he wanted to climb Everest "because it's there" that ought to be good enough for Paul Teasdale.

CHAPTER FIVE

PAUL PARKED THE JEEP in front of the little house where he and Sierra had first met. Josh collected his gear and said goodbye, then disappeared into a similar house next door. "Most of the houses around here were originally built by miners in the late 1800s or early 1900s," Paul said as he led Sierra inside. "They've been remodeled and updated, but the basic structure hasn't changed much."

The front room was furnished with a leather sofa, chair, bookshelves, an old trunk that doubled as a coffee table and a brass-trimmed woodstove in the corner. The bare wood floors and white-painted walls gave the room a clean, modern look, and large windows let in lots of light. A flat-screen TV sat in one corner and books filled the shelves and were piled on the trunk, along with numerous framed photographs.

"Let me stash my gear and I'll be right with you," Paul said, and went back outside to unload the Jeep.

Sierra moved to the bookshelf to study the photos there—Paul with grinning Sherpas, Paul and Josh on what might have been their trip to Everest, Paul with a puppy that must have been Indy, Paul with an attractive older couple—his parents?

Then she spotted the framed eight-by-ten at the back of the grouping and caught her breath. The man in the photo grinned at her with an expression as familiar as her own face in the mirror, and just as much a part of her.

She stared at the photograph of her father in his prime. She'd been there the day the photographer from *National Geographic* had visited their house. Her father was smiling at *her* in this picture—she was just off camera, making faces at him from behind the photographer's left shoulder.

She'd been nine, still at the stage where she thought of her dad as a superhero. He could do anything, from conquering distant mountains to fixing a flat on her bicycle. He'd lived at home for nine months before this photograph was taken, only going on short trips to speak about his exploits or to meet with sponsors of his next expedition. Sierra had grown used to the idea that he'd be with them forever, and even her mother was happier than Sierra could remember.

The day after the photographer left, their world fell apart again. Victor announced that *National Geographic* was sponsoring an expedition to Kilimanjaro, and he would leave the next week for four months.

"It's a good picture of him, don't you think?"

She hadn't heard Paul return to the house. He walked over to stand beside her. "He looks really relaxed and happy," he said.

She nodded, unable to speak. "He was looking at me when that picture was taken," she said. "He was smiling at *me.*"

She turned away from the photographs and walked to the sofa. "Should we get started with the interview?"

"We should have lunch first."

"I'm not hungry."

"After that climb, I am. Come on into the kitchen. You can talk to me while I fix us something to eat."

The kitchen was as simple and lovely as the living room, with cabinets painted a soft green and matching stone countertops. The deep sink might have been original to the house, though the side-by-side refrigerator was obviously newer.

She sat at the square wooden table and watched as he pulled various bowls and packages from the refrigerator and cabinets. She noted the full spice rack, various bottles of oils and marinades and the professional-quality cookware. "You cook," she said.

"When I have the time. I like to eat. Mountaineering food has come a long way since your father's day, but weeks of those freeze-dried rations really make a man appreciate fresh food."

She remembered a Sunday dinner: roast beef, mashed potatoes, green beans, sliced tomatoes, rolls and an enormous chocolate cake. "I dream about your cooking when I'm away," her father had told her mother when he'd finished eating. Her mother had beamed at him, though Sierra couldn't help think that it would have been far more romantic if he'd said he dreamed about her mother while he was away, and not merely her cooking.

Paul set part of a roast chicken, a container of hummus, a wedge of Swiss cheese, bread, crackers and various condiments on the table, then handed her a plate. "You might as well eat," he said. "There's plenty."

She put some hummus, cheese and crackers on her plate. "What's your favorite food?" she asked.

"Cheese enchiladas. I could eat them every day."

She made note of this. He laughed. "You're going to put that in your article?"

"I don't know. I won't know what I'll include until I sit down to write. I have an idea for how I want to shape the article, but you have to supply the details." She took out her tape recorder and set it in the middle of the table. "Starting now."

He stared at the recorder and took a long drink of water. He set down his glass and sat back in his chair. "My first big climb was Everest," he said. "I was eighteen, I'd just graduated high school and I hooked up with a group of tourists for a guided climb. The trip cost the equivalent of a semester's college tuition."

"What did your parents think of you spending that kind of money on a climb instead of college?"

"My mother cried. Not because she was upset about the money, but because she was worried I'd be hurt."

"Were *you* worried you'd be hurt?"

"Are you kidding? I was an eighteen-year-old guy. There's probably a survey somewhere that shows guys that age all think they're invincible."

"Do you still think you're invincible? Is that a quality necessary for mountain climbing?"

His expression sobered. "Climbing makes you very aware of your mortality," he said. "Brash climbers don't last long."

Finally they seemed to be getting somewhere with this interview. "Did something specific happen to teach you that lesson?" she asked.

"I realized later why they charged so much for that tourist climb," he said. "We were all so ignorant. I thought I had skills because I'd climbed a lot of fourteeners in Colorado and California, but I was as green as the rest." He shook his head. "We didn't even make it to the top because a storm blew in. After that, I decided to apprentice myself to someone who knew what he was doing. I signed on with George Gantry. He was your father's former partner, you know."

She nodded. She had memories of a large, loud man with wild blond hair like a lion's mane visiting the house and swooping her into his arms. "How about a kiss for Uncle George?" he'd shout. "What was George like to work for?" she asked.

"He was a tyrant. If you asked him that same question, he'd cheerfully agree. In exchange for a spot on his team, I got to be his slave—fetching and carrying and doing whatever he told me to do. But I learned a lot about climbing. George was a blowhard on flat land but on a mountain he had incredible skills. He told me your father had taught him everything."

"What kind of things?" she asked.

"How to read a mountain to find the best route. How to judge weather. How to push on through the tough patches." He leaned forward, expression intense. "People think climbing is all about the physical challenges, operating in thin air, steep slopes, unpredictable terrain and bad weather. But the real obstacles in climbing are the mental ones."

"Such as?"

He broke a cracker in half and contemplated the pieces. "There's a point in every climb when you want to quit. You're tired, everything hurts, your body is sick from not having enough oxygen. Maybe the food is getting to you, or the constant wind, or the stink of your own body from not having bathed in a week. You reach a point where you want to throw all your gear over the side of a cliff and go home."

"So why don't you?" she asked. "Why put yourself through all that?"

"Different people find different reasons. It could be a desire for fame, or the craving to see what the world looks like at the top, or wanting to beat out a competitor."

"Yes, but what drives you?" she asked.

He tossed the broken cracker aside. "I'm stubborn. I just hate to give up. I won't quit."

Sierra didn't try to hide her disappointment. "So climbing mountains is all about stubbornness? All that suffering and effort just so you can say you didn't quit?"

He laughed. "Hey, I never said I was deep. Every climber has something that gets them to the top. For me, it's obstinance."

She shook her head. "There has to be more to it than that. What made you so stubborn?"

"I can't help you there." He ate a cracker.

She tried another tack. "How did you end up working for George Gantry?"

"I asked him for a job. Begged, really."

"Why George?"

"Because he was one of the best climbers active at the time. And because he had been your father's partner."

Her father again. "It always comes back to my dad with you, doesn't it?"

"The climbing community isn't that large," Paul said. "At that time he'd only been dead a couple of years, so his influence was still felt. Most of his records were still intact. I'd made up my mind to be the best and if the best climber wasn't alive to teach me, I'd have to learn from the people he'd taught."

"You never met my father, so how is it he's exerted such a huge influence on your life?"

Paul shrugged. "There are some people we connect with, for whatever reason. Why does one person become mentor for another? Why are some people life-long enemies? Why do two people fall in love?" He shoved his half-empty plate aside. "What do you think your father would think about the two of us meeting?"

"I don't know what my father would think," she said. "I don't even know what I think." Her feelings about Paul were too mixed up with her feelings about her father. Being with Paul forced her to think more about her dad than she had in years, but Paul himself occupied another large portion of her thoughts. Her attraction to him was both inconvenient and unsettling.

PAUL STOOD AND BEGAN clearing the table, wishing for a way to clear the air between them. He hadn't thought his question about her father's thoughts on the two of them meeting was a particularly tough one, but the way Sierra clamped her mouth shut it was clear she hadn't liked it. Because she didn't think her father would approve? "Can I get you anything?" he asked. "I could make tea or coffee."

"I want you to sit down and answer my questions," she said. "I promise I won't bite."

"Wouldn't matter if you did. I've been inoculated for every disease known to man." Every one for which there was a vaccine, anyway.

He finished clearing the table, then sat opposite her. "Okay, fire away," he said.

"Tell me about your childhood. Where did you grow up?"

"Texas. I was born in Dallas, but I went to junior high and high school in Houston."

"Any brothers and sisters?"

"No. I'm an only child."

"When did you first become interested in mountain climbing?"

"When I saw that documentary I told you about— the British one about your father. I was fascinated. I taped it and watched it over and over." He had pretended he was with Victor Winston and his team, fighting the elements in pursuit of glory, far away from the trials of his own life and his personal Mount Everest.

"So that one documentary changed your life?" she asked.

He nodded. "I even wrote to your father. He wrote back and sent me that picture you were looking at."

"He wrote to you? A personal letter, or a canned response? He had a secretary who handled that kind of correspondence, you know."

"This was a personal letter, signed by him." Paul had been having a particularly rough time of it when the letter had arrived. Reading it, it was as if Victor had thrown him a lifeline to hang on to.

"Do you still have the letter?" Sierra asked. "Can I see it?"

"Sure." He went into his bedroom and took the

letter from the top drawer of the dresser and brought it back to her. "Careful," he said as he handed it to her. "It's getting pretty fragile after all these years."

The letter was short. He'd memorized the few lines of cramped script.

Dear Paul,

Thanks for writing to me. I was sorry to hear you've been ill, and I'm glad to know that watching me on television has helped in some small way in your recovery. I hope you'll continue to fight to get well. Once you've beaten your illness, conquering a mountain should be no problem for you. When I'm faced with difficulties during a climb, I find it helpful to keep my mind focused on my goal. The hardships and discomfort are merely things to be got through on my way to the top. They aren't what's really important.

I hope you are much better soon. Write and let me know.

Sincerely,

Victor Winston

Sierra looked up from the letter. "You were ill? What kind of illness?"

"I had cancer. Leukemia. It's why we moved from Dallas to Houston—to be near the M.D. Anderson Cancer Center."

Her face had gone pale. "So when you say you watched that documentary over and over…"

He nodded. "I had to spend a lot of time in bed. There wasn't much else to do. I was a bald, skinny, weak kid, but when I watched your father I could pretend I was strong enough to conquer mountains." For the duration of the show, at least, he could forget how afraid he was of dying.

"And obviously, you did get well."

"I had a bone-marrow transplant when I was four-teen. No more cancer." It sounded easy now, but he'd almost died twice during the process.

"That's amazing." She was writing now, her pen scribbling furiously across the page. "Did you write to my dad and let him know you were well?" she asked.

"I did. But he didn't answer." He'd told himself the letter must have gotten lost in the mail, but it was more likely that the famous Victor Winston didn't remember the boy who had sent him a letter two years before.

"Do you have any lingering health concerns now? Anything that interferes with your ability to climb?"

"None," he said. "I was lucky." Of course, any cancer patient, even one who was considered cured, lived with the possibility of a recurrence of the disease. Some studies had shown the chemotherapy and radia-tion used to treat childhood cancers could result in the development of new cancers as an adult.

It was one more thing that drove him. The cancer was a time bomb inside him, waiting to go off. Risking his life on mountains made it easier to deal with it, as if every time he faced down the possibility of his own demise, he got stronger, less afraid of the end. But he wouldn't share that with Sierra and her readers.

"So beating cancer led to your career as a mountaineer," she said.

"Yes."

She laid down her pencil and studied him. "I still don't understand," she said. "You cheated death once—why risk it over and over again?"

He shifted in his chair, trapped by her steady gaze. "Every time I stand on top of a mountain, it reminds me again how lucky I am to be alive," he said.

Sierra fumbled with her pen. The thought of Paul as a deathly ill boy who could only dream of climbing mountains brought a tightness to her chest. The image of Paul she'd come here with—brash, invincible, even arrogant—had been shattered by the reality of a much more complex man, alternately bold and vulnerable, aggravating and endearing. Now she had this picture of a sick boy to add to the collage.

"Why haven't I heard about this before?" she asked. "None of the news stories about you have mentioned it."

"I never told anyone before," he said. "It's not something I like to talk about."

"But you told me."

"I hadn't planned to, but...you're Victor's daughter. I never had the opportunity to tell him how much he helped me get through that bad time, but I can at least tell you."

She focused on her notebook, struggling to process conflicting emotions. She was touched that Paul would confide in her, but disappointed he'd done so only because of her father.

As if to prove this further, Paul said. "My one regret is that I never got to meet Victor. I saw his public persona, in the documentaries and magazine articles, but what was he like at home, with you and your mother?"

Like Paul and his illness, Sierra's father was a subject she didn't like to talk about. But he'd shared that part of himself with her, so to keep the conversation going, she would return the favor.

"When I was very small, he wasn't famous yet, and he didn't climb full-time. He did seasonal construction work and climbed during vacations and slow times. I don't think he was as driven then."

"So he was pretty much a regular guy," Paul said.

"He really didn't start to be known as an alpinist until I was seven or eight. After that, he was gone a lot more. He and my mother separated when I was ten and after that I didn't see him as much."

"What do you remember most about those early days?" Paul asked.

"I remember that we were happy. He smiled a lot

then. He had one of those smiles that really transformed his face, so that he was almost handsome."

"Was he not as happy later?"

She shook her head. "The more mountains he conquered, the more serious and intense he became." His
focus shrank to include less and less of the world
around him, so that at the end, he'd shut out even
those closest to him.

The letter her father had written to Paul had been
an unexpected glimpse of a man she'd almost forgotten had existed. She tried to imagine him composing
his reply to the sick little boy, but couldn't.

Victor had grown more callous in his later years, a
judgment confirmed by the fact that he'd never bothered to answer Paul's second letter.

"I'm sorry to hear that," Paul said. "Climbing is in
many ways such a solitary pursuit. Even when you're
part of a large team, conditions make conversation
difficult, and each person is responsible for himself.
Your focus is all on yourself, on mustering that extra
bit of strength and will to keep going. Coming back
into a world where you interact with other people can
be jarring."

"You don't seem to have any difficulty," she said.
From what she'd seen, Paul had many friends and was
well-liked.

"I like people," he said. "But I can be satisfied with
my own company, too."

Satisfied with his own company. "I guess you spent

a lot of time alone when you had your bone-marrow transplant," she said.

He nodded. "The treatment requires several days of isolation, and very limited contact with others for several weeks after that. I guess you could say that it was training for the solo climbs that have become my specialty."

She copied the quote into her notebook. "This is going to be a great story," she said.

"Just don't forget that my illness isn't the whole story," he said.

"Right. So what's the rest of the story?"

"I'm still writing it," he said.

"What are your plans? What do you hope your legacy will be?"

He shifted in his chair and looked uncomfortable. "I'm a little young to be thinking about a legacy," he said. "One other thing my illness taught me was to not worry about the future. My focus is on right now, today." He glanced out the window. "It's a beautiful day out. Want to drive into Montrose with me to pick up a few things I need?"

"I don't think so." The revelations of the afternoon had left her feeling too emotionally vulnerable to spend any more time with him than necessary. "I guess you're telling me the interview is over?"

"I told you before, I'm a lot more comfortable doing than talking, especially about myself," he said. "Besides, aren't you sick of hearing about me?"

On the contrary, she found him fascinating, but she kept this information to herself. She closed her notebook and clicked her pen shut. "I suppose I have enough material for one afternoon." She stowed the tape recorder in her purse. "It will take me a few hours to transcribe the tape and organize my notes, then I'll have a better idea of what I still need."

"That doesn't sound like a fun way to spend the evening. Why don't you come out with me, instead?"

His tone was casual, yet his gaze locked on her. "Are you asking me on a date?" she asked.

"Why not? There's a band tonight at The Outlaw."

She could think of half a dozen reasons she shouldn't go out with him, starting with the fact that she was supposed to be interviewing him for an article and ending with her leaving town in four days. She'd come to Ouray to work, not get personally involved with her interview subject. But considering how much time she'd spent not interviewing Paul and the personal things they'd each confided, they were clearly more than coolly distant reporter and subject.

Bottom line—she liked Paul, but she didn't know what she should do about those feelings. Since she was leaving soon, what was the point in taking things any further?

On the other hand, was she passing up the opportunity for something great?

"I really do have to work," she said, half-hoping he'd try harder to talk her into coming with him.

"Suit yourself." He stood. "I'll drive you back to the hotel."

"No, thanks. I can walk."

"Are you sure? You looked a little winded this morning."

"I'd rather walk." She needed the exercise to clear her head and organize her thoughts.

"All right, then." He walked her to the door. "Should I kiss you goodbye?"

His tone was teasing and his eyes flashed with amusement, so she tried to adopt the same attitude with her reply, though her heart beat erratically at the thought of his lips on hers again. "That won't be necessary," she said.

"Can't blame a guy for trying." He held open the door. "That's something else I learned from my time in the hospital."

"Kissing or trying?"

"Never pass up the opportunity for pleasure," he said.

It was almost enough to make her turn around and kiss him. Almost, but her sense of dignity held her back. What if this was all just a joke to him? She'd never felt she was good at reading men, especially a man like Paul, whose cavalier attitude concealed such depths. She hadn't inherited her father's love of risk, especially when it came to exposing her emotions, so she didn't turn back and kiss Paul. Instead she started down the hill toward her hotel, aware of him watching her all the way to Main Street.

CHAPTER SIX

BACK AT THE HOTEL, Sierra found Kelly in the bar. "I've got that list of contacts in New York for you," Sierra said. She'd made the list last night. "Come up when you get the chance."

"I can come up now." Kelly looked around the almost empty bar. "The lunch rush is over and I've got time to kill before I have to get ready for the happy-hour crowd."

She followed Sierra up the stairs and down the hall to her room. "Did you find Paul?" Kelly asked as she waited for Sierra to unlock her door.

"Yes. He was at the hot springs. Thanks for pointing me there."

"Did you have any luck getting him to answer your questions?"

"Yes. We had a good interview." She was still reeling from the revelation about Paul's cancer. He was obviously so strong and healthy now, it was hard to imagine him as a sick little boy.

She retrieved some papers from the desk and handed them to Kelly. "The first sheet is a rental agent and a couple of private individuals who can help you find a place to live. The top name on the second page is a talent agent I know, and the other two names are people who might help you get a job."

Kelly scanned the pages. "Thank you! Thank you so much!"

"They're only names. And they may not be all that much help."

"I'm sure they will be. Keith will be so excited."

"Keith?"

"My boyfriend. I'd love for you to meet him."

"I'd like that." She was curious to meet the man who was willing to finance Kelly's move away from him. "Do you think he'll come to New York with you?" she asked.

"I don't see how he can," Kelly said. "I mean, he has a business here."

"That must be kind of hard, huh—leaving him?"

Kelly shrugged. "It is, but hey, I can't let that stand in the way of my dream, right? I mean, Keith's giving me this chance and I'd be a fool not to take it."

"Right." If she'd been in Kelly's shoes, she'd surely have done the same, but did she have to be so, well, *cold?*

"Hey, we're going over to The Outlaw tonight to hear The Railbenders," Kelly said. "They're a really kickin' band from Denver. You should stop by. Then you could meet Keith."

"Thanks, but I really have a lot of work to do."

"Paul will probably be there."

Paul, around whom she felt entirely too vulnerable. Not only had he unearthed the childhood memories of her father that she'd never shared with anyone else, but he constantly distracted her from her purpose here. The more time she spent with him, the less she saw him as merely an interview subject, and the more she cared about him as a man. "Thank you, but I really need to work on this article."

"Suit yourself," Kelly said. "But if you change your mind, it's right down the street."

"Thanks." Some time alone with the facts of Paul's life would no doubt remind her of all the reasons she should continue to fight her attraction to him.

She booted up her laptop, then switched on the tape recorder. She spent the next couple of hours transcribing the interview tape and organizing her notes. Paul's voice, calm and low, filled the room. When she came to the part of their conversation where he talked about his cancer and the letter her father had sent, tears welled in her eyes. She blinked them away, but she couldn't as easily put away her sadness over a boy who had almost died, and a girl who missed the closeness she'd once known with her dad.

Her father was the other important part of this story. Before she could write about Paul, she needed to sketch a summary of the events leading to her father's death—a mini history to bring readers up-to-date. She knew the facts from the newspaper, but those stories had focused on the climb itself and the efforts to rescue Victor once he was trapped by the storm. She needed to know what had led her father to make the solo climb in the first place. Her own memories of that time were too hazy. She needed more information.

With a feeling of dread knotting her stomach, she hit speed dial for her mother. Jennifer Richardson— she'd reverted to her maiden name after Victor's death—hadn't been pleased when Sierra had told her she was going to interview the man who had found Victor's body. "He should have left him up there on McKinley," she said. "Victor wasted so much of his life on the slope of one mountain or another. Why shouldn't he spend eternity there?"

"Hello?" Her mother's voice was sleepy, though it was only a little after nine at her home in New Jersey. "Hello?"

"Hi, Mom. It's me, Sierra."

"Of course it's you. You don't think I have a bunch of other daughters running around, do you?" Sierra heard fumbling, and the clink of ice in a glass. Her stomach tightened further.

"How are you doing, Mom?" she asked.

"I'm fine. I took your grandmother to the doctor today. She needs surgery on her other hip, but she refuses to have it. She'd rather complain to me and Dad. He just turns off his hearing aid when she starts in, but I'm not so lucky."

Sierra pictured the house both she and her mother

had grown up in—a sprawling, elegant estate in rural New Jersey, built by Jennifer's father, Adam Richardson, when she'd been a baby. Sierra and her mother had retreated there when Jennifer left Victor. For a while, Sierra had imagined they'd move to their own place soon, perhaps a little house nearby—though the only little houses in that neighborhood were guest cottages or servants' quarters.

But Jennifer had settled into her childhood home and stayed. Sierra didn't believe her mother was really happy there, only that she didn't have the energy to uproot herself once more.

"Where are you?" her mother demanded. "I tried to call you yesterday and your office said you were on assignment. You didn't answer at your apartment, either."

"You should've tried my cell."

"Two phone calls to try to locate my daughter are enough. Where were you?"

"I'm still in Colorado. You remember—I'm doing a story about Paul Teasdale." She winced at the sound of a glass set down hard on the table beside the phone. She hoped her mother wasn't about to launch into one of her tirades against her father, or mountaineering in general.

"What's he like?" Jennifer asked instead.

"Paul?"

"No, the abominable snowman. Of course, Paul. What's the young Turk of Mountaineering like?"

"He's…he's interesting. Not what I expected."

"Good-looking?"

"Yes, I guess you could say he was good-looking."

Her mother laughed. "You're not sure, or you don't want to tell me?"

"I said he was good-looking, okay?"

"I remember the first time I saw your father. Nobody would call him handsome, but there was just something about him… First time he walked into a party I was attending, I felt he'd sucked all the air out of the room. I couldn't even breathe, I was so captivated by him."

This revelation startled Sierra—not that her mother had been captured by her father's famous charisma, but that Jennifer would admit it. "I can breathe just fine around Paul," she said. Any light-headedness she felt was strictly due to the altitude.

Jennifer was obviously in a nostalgic mood tonight, whether because she'd so recently buried her husband or from the vodka that no doubt filled the glass clinking against the phone as she raised it to her lips. "Every woman in that room was jealous when he asked me to dance," she continued. "If you'd asked me before that night if I believed in love at first sight, I'd have laughed you out of the house. But that's what happened. One dance and I was done for."

Sierra hadn't heard this story before. She was fascinated, craving more, but afraid of breaking whatever spell her mother was under. "You got engaged pretty quickly, didn't you?" she prompted.

"In one week." Jennifer laughed, a sloppy chuckle. "Your grandfather was furious. But I was too much in love to care."

"What was it about Dad that attracted you so much?" Sierra asked.

"He had a great sense of humor. He made me laugh. And he was confident. He knew exactly what he wanted to do with his life. That kind of confidence is incredibly sexy."

Paul had that kind of confidence. Her mom was right—it was very sexy.

"And he was really strong," Jennifer said. "Not just physically, but mentally. Strong enough to stand up to my father, which no one ever did. I thought he was strong enough to protect me forever."

Protect you from what? Sierra wanted to ask, but Jennifer was crying now and Sierra felt bad about upsetting her. "It's okay, Mom," she said. "You should take it easy. Watch a little TV and go to bed." *Don't drink so much.* But mentioning the drinking only made her mother angry and inclined to drink that much more. "Good night, Mom," she said.

"Good night, darling. Come home soon. Stay away from that man. Mountain climbers are no good. He'll only leave you to climb some damn mountain. It's a sickness, and you can't cure it, no matter how hard you try."

"I know, Mom. I'll be okay, I promise." She hung up and tucked the phone away once more. She hadn't gotten around to asking her mother for the information for her article; she'd look later on the Internet. This meant that whatever she wrote, it would only be external facts, not the emotions behind the events. She'd never be able to show how in dying on that mountain, her father had not only destroyed himself, but the once vivacious young woman who had married him so impulsively and followed him for years. Jennifer had found the strength to leave Victor, but she'd never stopped loving him; even now, she wasn't able to let go.

The thought of losing herself to another person that way terrified Sierra, and made her angry. Paul was not her father, though he shared many of his better qualities—strength and humor and the ability to make others care about his own passions. But he also suffered from an obsession with mountains—that sickness, as her mother called it.

That sickness was why Sierra was here in Ouray, she reminded herself. And it was surely enough to keep her immune to Paul's charms.

She shut down the laptop and checked the clock—barely eight. She could turn on the television and watch a bad sitcom, or try to focus on the novel she'd brought with her.

Or she could find The Outlaw Saloon and face Paul—and her fears.

THE OUTLAW WAS PACKED with people of all ages—
mostly locals, with a few tourists mixed in. As Paul
worked his way through the crush, he was greeted by
many familiar faces. "Hey, Paul, great to see you!"
"Paul! Glad you could make it." "You owe me a dance,
Paul." This last from a cute blonde named Charla who
worked the front desk of the Beaumont Hotel.

Paul nodded and waved and kept working his way
toward the edge of the dance floor, where Josh had
staked out a table. "I knew you'd be here," Josh said
as Paul pulled out a chair. Two other climbing buddies
and their girlfriends shared the table. Paul greeted
them all and ordered a beer from a passing waitress.

"You didn't bring Sierra with you?" Josh asked.

"She said she had too much work to do."

"Work?" Josh looked disgusted. "That's a pretty
lame excuse."

"She takes her job seriously." He felt the need to
defend Sierra. Yes, she could be a little standoffish, but
underneath that big-city aloofness was a sensitive,
caring woman. One he wished was with him tonight.

The band took the stage and people poured onto the
dance floor. Charla made her way over to Paul and
grabbed his hand. "Let's dance," she said.

"Sure." He led Charla onto the dance floor and into
a quick two-step. She was cute and fun, the music was
good and there was no reason he shouldn't have a
good time tonight and forget all about Sierra Winston.

The song ended and he started to lead Charla back

to his table when he glimpsed a familiar figure out of the corner of his eye and froze.

Sierra stood on the edge of the room, scanning the crowd. Was she looking for him?

He spotted Josh with two other men near the edge of the stage. He led Charla to them. "Josh, you know Charla, don't you?" he said.

Josh grinned at the petite blonde. "I've seen you around," he said. "Nice to meet you."

"I have to, uh, see someone about something," Paul said, giving Josh a significant look. *Bail me out here, buddy,* the look said.

"Charla and I will be just fine," Josh said. He put a hand on Charla's shoulder. "Can I buy you a drink?"

She glanced at Paul, who was already backing away, then turned the full force of her smile on Josh. "I'd love one," she said, and settled into the chair beside him.

Paul found Sierra in the same spot, still searching the crowd. She wore jeans and a sapphire-blue top made of a silky fabric that clung to her curves, sleeveless to show off her slender arms. "I'm glad you changed your mind about coming here," he said, slipping up beside her.

She flushed. "I decided it would round out my article to show you doing something besides climbing and hiking." Would it also help her to see him as more than just an assignment?

He suddenly wished they were anywhere but this

crowded club. The loud music made extended conversation impossible, and the crush of people around them erased any possibility of time alone. The best he could hope for was to hold her in his arms on the dance floor. "Would you like to dance?" he asked.

"I would."

They threaded their way to the dance floor, her hand in his, and joined the shuffling, twirling, swaying couples. He spotted Josh and Charla and breathed a sigh of relief. She was laughing at something Josh had said, too engaged to notice Paul and Sierra.

They had been dancing only a few seconds when the lively rocker segued into a slower number. Paul pulled Sierra closer. She didn't protest, merely settled against him. "You're a good dancer," she said.

"Thanks. I took lessons when I was in high school."

"Really? I didn't think dance was very popular with teenage boys."

"After I finished the treatments for cancer, I was pretty skinny and weak. My mom thought dancing would be a good way to build up my strength, while improving my social skills at the same time."

"And did it?"

"It's a decent way to get in shape. But Mom didn't realize that teenage boys in dance classes are as rare as hen's teeth. My only partners were women old enough to be my mother—or grandmother."

She laughed. "Then why did you stick with it?"

"I didn't want to hurt my mom's feelings." She'd

aged ten years during his illness and still seemed so fragile. "Besides, I like to dance." To emphasize the point, he led her in a twirl, followed by a dip.

She faltered only a little, then was back in his arms, eyes shining. "Did you take lessons, too?" he asked.

"No. Which explains why I'm not very good."

"You're doing great." He settled his hand more firmly on her hip and pressed even closer. He wanted to know everything about her—what she did and what she felt and what she hoped for. "Where did you live growing up?" he asked. "I know Victor started in California—did you spend most of your childhood there?"

She nodded. "Until my parents split up when I was ten. Then my mother and I went to live with her parents in New Jersey."

"That must have been a culture shock."

"It was. I'd grown up in relatively small towns in the mountains and suddenly we were in a suburb of Princeton. Everything looked different, sounded different, tasted different."

"I was twelve when we moved from Dallas to Houston," he said. "It wasn't as big a change, but it was hard being the new kid, leaving all my friends behind." In and out of the hospital for treatments, he hadn't had much opportunity to make new friends, which was maybe one more reason he'd fixated on Victor Winston and mountain climbing.

"Did you miss your father?" he asked.

She nodded. "Terribly. For a while, I blamed my mother for leaving him, but she kept insisting that he was the one who'd left us—that he'd chosen his precious mountains over us. After a while—when he called and visited less and less—I saw that was true."

Paul sensed the anguish behind those words. Anger at Victor made him clench his jaw. It was one thing not to answer a letter from a boy he didn't know, but how could the man have treated his own daughter this way?

"My grandparents didn't help matters," Sierra continued. "They'd never wanted my mother to marry my father in the first place. Now they were angry that he'd hurt her, and they didn't censor their feelings around me."

"Maybe that was why your father didn't visit much—because he wasn't welcome."

"I was still his daughter. Their attitude shouldn't have made a difference if he wanted to see me."

"You're right. It shouldn't have." Paul wouldn't have let others' disappointment keep him away from the people he loved, but maybe Victor was a weaker man than Paul thought.

The song ended and she moved out of his arms. "Let's sit down for a minute," she said.

PAUL DIDN'T FEEL comfortable returning to the table where Charla now sat with Josh, so he looked for a vacant seat. He spotted two empty chairs at a table with Kelly and her boyfriend, Keith.

"Are these seats taken?" he asked.

"Hey, Paul! Sierra!" Kelly jumped up. "Keith, you remember Paul, don't you? And this is Sierra Winston. She's the reporter from New York I was telling you about. This is Keith MacIntyre, from Telluride."

Keith stood and shook hands. Tall and angular, he was older than the others at the table, maybe late thirties. With his neatly trimmed goatee, manicured hands and crisply pressed shirt, he looked like someone who would be right at home with Telluride's moneyed celebrities, yet there was nothing snobby about him. He had a salesman's firm handshake and warm smile, but didn't come across as phony. "Nice to meet you," he said, and nodded to Sierra.

"Nice to meet you, too," she said. Paul held a chair for her, and she turned to him. "I need to excuse myself to visit the ladies' room," she said.

"I'll come with you," Kelly said.

Paul watched the two women until they were swallowed up by the crowd.

Love. Was *that* what Paul was feeling for Sierra— this dreamlike sensation that had him feeling so uncertain and off-kilter lately?

"So, WHAT DO YOU THINK of Keith?" Kelly asked as she and Sierra touched up their makeup before the mirror in the ladies' room.

"Oh, um, he seems very nice." What could she say about a man she'd seen all of thirty seconds?

"He's the most wonderful man I've ever met." Kelly smiled at her reflection.

Sierra stared at her younger friend. Kelly seemed different tonight—softer. Her black tank top, tight black jeans and stiletto heels were on the cutting edge of fashion, as were her bright red lips and nails. She looked like the same ambitious, driven woman Sierra had connected with her first night in town. But the edgy restlessness Sierra had recognized before was missing tonight, replaced by a dreamy-eyed wistfulness. "What's going on?" she asked. "Did something special happen tonight?"

"Is it that obvious?" Kelly turned to her, smiling. "Keith told me he loved me. He said it right out loud, without me saying it first. Can you believe it?"

"That's wonderful." Everyone wanted to be loved, right? But could such a simple declaration account for Kelly's transformation? "Did anything else happen?" Sierra asked.

"Isn't that enough? I never had a guy say he loved me before—well, not when he really meant it. Not when I hadn't said it first."

Sierra wouldn't have thought Kelly was the kind of woman who gave her heart away easily, but then, how well did she really know the girl? Maybe Sierra was only projecting her own personality onto Kelly because of the supposed connection she'd felt between them.

She realized Kelly was still looking at her, as if expecting a reply. "Congratulations," Sierra said. "I'm really happy for you." Maybe even a little envious. After years of dating, Sierra was beginning to think she was impervious to love. Would she even recognize the feeling when it came along? "Does this change your plans to move to New York?" she asked.

"Change my plans?" Kelly's eyes widened. "I've wanted to move to New York for years. Why would I change my mind now?"

"I thought you might have decided to stay here with Keith."

Kelly shook her head, her hair swinging from side to side with the force of the movement. "He would never ask me to do that. I can't give up my dream for a man. You wouldn't do something like that, would you?"

"Of course not." No man was worth changing her whole life for. But what did she really know? She'd never been in the position to have to choose.

"Keith understands why I need to leave," Kelly said. "He'd never try to hold me back." Her expression grew dreamy once more. "Yet he loves me anyway, even though he knows I'm leaving. Isn't that the most romantic thing you ever heard of?"

Romantic—or foolish? Sierra doubted the strength of Keith's love if he was so willing to let Kelly abandon him for the sake of untested ambition.

Then again, maybe the answer wasn't that Keith's

love wasn't strong enough, but that Kelly's dreams were stronger. That kind of drive had taken Sierra's father away from his family, but it had also taken Sierra to New York and the top of her profession.

"I'm sure I'll miss him when I leave," Kelly said. "But he can come visit me. Maybe we'll have a long-distance romance. That could be exciting."

More frustrating than exciting, Sierra thought. "Do you think you'll miss Ouray?" she asked.

Kelly shrugged. "Do you miss where you grew up?"

"No. Manhattan is my home now." She had a job she loved, a nice apartment and good friends. Maybe that wasn't enough for some people—for them, home meant family, but Sierra told herself she couldn't miss what she didn't really have.

Her father had cut his ties with his family. Had he done so to free himself to conquer whichever mountain next claimed his attention, without having to consider the feelings of those left behind?

Did Paul feel that way? He didn't have a girlfriend, and her research had turned up no hint that he'd ever come close to marrying or even living with someone. Did he avoid such entanglements in order to remain free to pursue the kind of fame her father had achieved?

In the end, fame hadn't saved her father from dying alone, and had only added to Sierra and her mother's suffering. Maybe Paul was smart to avoid dragging other people along with him on his journey. Maybe he was, as he'd said, "content in his own skin."

But it sounded terribly lonely to Sierra. As lonely as her own life was beginning to feel.

"I'm telling myself to just enjoy the moment and not worry too much about the future," Kelly said. "I'm going to move to New York to be an actress and Keith knows and accepts that. We'll enjoy each other while we can and not think about the rest."

"I guess that's a good way to handle it," Sierra said. Her father had once sworn in an interview that the best way to survive a grueling high-altitude climb was to avoid thinking past the next step. Maybe the same approach applied to relationships.

"Speaking of romance, you and Paul looked pretty cozy on the dance floor," Kelly said.

Cozy was a good word for it. Safe in his arms. Not that she needed to be protected from anything, but the idea of having someone there for her if she needed him was comforting. "He's a good dancer."

"He is that." Kelly stashed her makeup bag in her purse. "Come on. They're going to think we fell in."

They returned to their table, and Sierra studied Keith. He didn't look like her idea of a sugar daddy. And he was obviously besotted with Kelly. Besotted enough to let her leave? Or did he think that if he let her go, she'd come back? It was a nice sentiment, but Sierra doubted it worked in real life. Her mother had let her father go and he stayed gone. Then she left him and he never tried to get her back.

In spite of all this, Sierra was sure her parents had

loved each other. Love was supposed to be such a positive emotion, but it also had the power to make people so sad. As difficult as it was to be alone sometimes, Sierra thought loneliness was preferable to heartbreak. She'd avoided that hazard so far by always choosing men she could be friends with, like Mark. No fiery breakups for her, no agonizing heartaches.

She glanced at Paul, who was laughing at something Kelly had said. Their eyes met, and she felt a sharp pull deep in her chest. It wasn't a painful feeling exactly, but she sensed it had the potential to hurt, if she let him get any closer.

CHAPTER SEVEN

PAUL MOVED HIS CHAIR closer to Sierra. He'd noticed that she'd been staring at him. At first, he'd thought he had something in his hair, or that she wanted to ask him something. But this look had been different, almost…tender. The same way he often felt about her—he wanted to make up for the hurt she'd suffered and to protect her from further injury. And if he couldn't stand between her and all the injuries the world could wreak, he at least wanted to stand beside her. It was a crazy idea, considering how hard he'd worked to remain independent, but the more time he spent with Sierra, the more he liked the thought of the two of them as a couple.

The band began a lively number and Kelly jumped up and tugged at Keith's hand. "I love this song," she said. "We have to dance."

"Do you want to dance?" Paul asked Sierra.

She shook her head. "Let's just talk."

"All right. What would you like to talk about?"

"You said you'd climbed mountains near here—some of the ones we saw the other day."

"Yeah. I've climbed most of them a few times."

"Do you think I could climb any of them?"

"There are a few pretty easy ones. Sure."

"Will you climb one of them with me? This week?"

He couldn't hold back a grin at this surprising turn of events. "We could do that. But why the change of heart? I had to practically beg to get you to go above tree line in a Jeep."

"I've changed my mind. It will be good research for my article."

Was that the only reason she wanted to do this? Research? "That's what I call dedication. But you know, even an easy climb isn't like a walk across town."

"I want to know what it's like." She spread one hand flat on the tabletop, fingers splayed. She had long, delicate fingers, the nails polished a pearly pink—not the hands of a climber. "Maybe if I make it to the top, I'll understand what the attraction is for you—what it was for my dad," she said.

That old hurt was in her voice, the one he wanted to take away. He smoothed his hand down her arm. "I'd be honored to take you." He'd never climbed with a woman before, not even one of the nontechnical fourteeners nearby. It seemed appropriate that Sierra would be the first, and not only because she was Victor Winston's daughter. He felt close to Sierra, even though he'd known her only a few days. He'd shared his past with her, and now he wanted to share this experience, too.

"We can do Uncompahgre Peak. You won't need any special equipment for that one. You can walk right up to the top."

"When?"

"How about Friday?"

"All right. Thanks." Her smile was faint. "I'm a little nervous."

"Don't be. You'll have a great time. And I won't let anything happen to you." He took her hand and squeezed it, then kept holding it. He didn't want to let Sierra go.

SIERRA HAD PROPOSED the mountain climbing expedition in a moment of bravado, hoping the outing would help clarify her emotions about mountains and her father and Paul. Maybe she'd hate it and decide both men were certifiable nuts that she wanted nothing to do with. Maybe she'd love the experience and understand their mania.

Most likely, her feelings would fall somewhere in between, but maybe on the long walk up the mountain she'd find a way to reconcile the love and hate that pulled at her.

Paul left Sierra on her own Thursday. She'd planned to use the time to work on her article, but she was too nervous and excited to sit at a desk for eight hours.

Mark had urged her to relax and treat the time in Ouray as a vacation. The area had its share of tourist activities, if one was into visiting old mines or photographing ghost-town ruins. These held little appeal for her, which left one other activity she always enjoyed—shopping.

While Paul was doing whatever he needed to prepare for their climb, Sierra would make some preparations of her own. She hadn't missed the edge of doubt in his voice last night when he'd asked if she was sure she wanted to make the climb.

He thought she was a city girl in over her head. She'd prove him wrong by showing up tomorrow properly equipped for their climb. Ouray might not have a mall, but she was pretty sure she could find everything she needed for any kind of outdoor activity in one of the shops on Main Street.

An hour later, Sierra was the proud owner of something called a hydration pack—a backpack with a water bladder and a flexible tube to sip from—a pair of adjustable trekking poles, a fleece jacket and a fetching broad-brimmed hat. The clerk had assured her she'd look like a pro when she set out in the morning.

She was definitely no amateur when it came to scoping out the offerings at Ouray's other shops. Though the town was small, she was delighted to find some first-class offerings. By early afternoon she had scored a hand-blown Christmas ornament, a tooled leather belt and Belgian chocolate truffles. At an old-fashioned variety store that was stuffed to the rafters with everything from canning jars to casting reels, she bought a disposable camera with which to record tomorrow's accomplishments, as well as a goofy-faced ceramic bear paperweight for Mark. He would love it.

Laden with packages and feeling more relaxed than she had since leaving New York, she stopped for lunch at O'Brien's Pub. The hostess showed her to a table on the patio and she settled back with a sigh. She wondered how Paul had spent his day so far. Some time apart from him had seemed like a sensible idea this morning, but she'd missed his lanky figure at her side and his goofy jokes. She missed his intense brown eyes studying her and his hand reaching out to steady her at an uneven place on the sidewalk. Such little gestures made her feel cared for—an unfamiliar, yet not unwelcome, sensation.

"Hey! Looks like you've been doing your part to stimulate the local economy." Paul's climbing buddy, Josh, stopped by her table. He wore what she'd come to think of as the uniform of the Ouray male—hiking shorts, T-shirt advertising some local attraction, band or beer, and boots. But Josh wore his clothes with a little extra flair—the T-shirt newer, the shorts crisper. Sierra decided he knew he was good-looking and played that to his advantage.

"I'm having fun exploring the local stores," she said.

"Mind if I join you for lunch?" He indicated the empty chair across from her.

"Not at all."

They ordered burgers and soft drinks. Josh flirted with the waitress, who returned his banter with equanimity. Sierra gathered they had known each other a long time—though maybe the smallness of the town and its relative isolation from the rest of the world accelerated the pace of relationships.

"What do you do?" she asked him when they were alone once more. "I mean, for a living?" Why did he have so much free time on an August afternoon?

"I teach history and geography at the local high school."

"Ah." She nodded. Such a normal, adult profession. She'd assumed Josh, like Paul, had some unconventional job as a fishing guide or a climbing instructor—work that didn't interfere with climbing, hiking or other outdoor pursuits.

"Have you seen Paul this morning?" Josh asked.

"No. Have you?"

"Not since last night. I figured he was busy with you. How are the interviews going?"

"All right." She still had questions to ask Paul, but her sense of urgency was gone. Instead of leaving town early, as she had planned, she found herself contemplating ways of drawing out her visit, to spend a little more time with Paul. "Did I interrupt anything yesterday?" she asked. "Did the two of you have plans to do more climbing?"

"Nah. Paul was just helping me set a course for

some kids from Children's Hospital that are coming to town."

"Oh?"

"Yeah, it's an adventure trip for critically ill children. They're going to raft a river, have a cookout and take a Jeep tour. Here in Ouray they'll climb the pool wall if they want to, then play in the hot-springs pool."

"And you and Paul are helping with this?" A dangerous surge of sentimentality filled her.

"I'm helping. Paul declined to volunteer—I don't think he's comfortable around kids."

Or maybe it was only sick children he wanted to avoid. Did Josh know about Paul's cancer? "How long have you two known each other?" she asked.

"Six years? We met at the Ice Park before he moved to Ouray. I broke an ice axe and he let me borrow one of his."

"So you'd say he was a generous guy."

"Oh, yeah—he'd give you the shirt off his back. He's not much into material possessions." Josh shook ketchup onto his plate. "He takes care of his equipment, because that's his livelihood, but he doesn't care about clothes or cars or anything like that."

"Does he not care, or is it just that he likes to travel light? No ties, no possessions, he can pick up and move whenever he wants."

Josh considered the question. "Maybe. I never thought about it one way or another." He shrugged. "One thing about trekking—when you have to carry everything you need in a pack on your back or pulled behind you on a sled, you learn pretty quick what you can do without. It's one reason why I gave it up. I like my comforts."

"I'm with you there. I'm not into suffering." Paul clearly enjoyed a nice home, beautiful surroundings and good meals. So what drove him to leave all that for the deprivations of a high-altitude climb? It was one of the puzzles about climbing she was still no closer to understanding.

"Paul and I are hoping to climb Uncompahgre Peak tomorrow," she said.

"It's a nice hike," Josh said. "You'll like it."

For Sierra, a nice hike was a stroll through Central Park. Uncompahgre Peak was over fourteen thousand feet above sea level, up where the air was thin and no trees grew. "I'm a little nervous," she said. "I've never climbed a mountain before."

"You'll be fine. Remember to drink lots of water, and take it slow. And you'll be with an expert. You'll have a good time."

Mountains and a good time were not words that went together in her mind, but she wanted to do this. She wanted to experience a little of what her father had known. What Paul knew. "You don't think I'm being overly ambitious for my first time?" she asked.

"No. You'll do great. Hey, I have a climbing joke for you."

"All right."

"Two guys are climbing and one admires the other's new ice axe. 'What'd you pay for that?' he asks.

"'Nothing,' the first guy says. 'I was climbing the other day and this beautiful woman walked up, threw down her tools, stripped off her climbing suit and said I could have anything I wanted.'

"'Good choice,' the second guy said. 'Her climbing suit would have never fit you.'"

She laughed, but her mirth had a bitter edge. If given the opportunity, would Paul choose climbing over everything else? She knew what her father had answered. So far, Paul had certainly put climbing first in his life, but would he ever allow something else—some*one* else—to take precedence?

She thought of Kelly, for whom love wasn't enough to sway her from her ambition, and of her own single-mindedness as she'd climbed the ladder of her career. In Sierra's case, ambition hadn't been the only thing driving her. Work had been a way to fight loneliness, a way to make a place for herself in a new and unfamiliar city.

Even before she came west she'd been restless. She wanted to make a change, but didn't know what that change might be. Her father's reemergence in the news and in her life, combined with her talks with Paul, had made her think about the importance of family and connections with other people.

Maybe she was ready to find someone and make a

life with him. But it would have to be the right man, one who wouldn't leave, the way her father had. She wouldn't make her mother's mistake and try to hold on to a man for whom she could only ever be a second love.

EXCEPT WHEN ON an expedition, or representing one of his sponsors at a trade show or other function, Paul rarely planned his days. He woke each morning and decided then how he would spend the next few hours. In exchange for a discount on the rent, he performed maintenance on the old house and on two others his landlord owned. Some days he climbed or hiked. He researched mountains and climbing routes, made the occasional trip to Montrose or Grand Junction to purchase supplies, answered e-mail from fans and friends, or spent days reading or watching TV. He tried to enjoy every day, however it unfolded.

Sierra had interrupted the easy rhythm of his life. He blamed her questions and her unsettling presence for the new restlessness that plagued him.

After dropping her off at her hotel on Wednesday night, he'd tossed and turned for hours before drifting into a fitful sleep. He woke late Thursday morning, roused from sleep by Indy's whines, and stumbled into the kitchen to make coffee and feed the dog. As he sipped his coffee and his head cleared, he stared out the window at the rocky slope rising behind the house and thought, not of climbing, but of Sierra. What was she doing this morning? Should he seek her out and ask her to go hiking with him? They could do something easy this time, like the Perimeter Trail around town. She'd enjoy the views, and afterward they could visit the hot springs, and talk about tomorrow's climb of Uncompahgre Peak.

He turned his back to the window, wishing he could turn away as easily from his thoughts. He'd expected to like Sierra because she was Victor's daughter, but he hadn't expected to fall in love with her. Maybe love was too strong a word for feelings toward someone he'd known only three days, but he definitely felt a connection with Sierra that was stronger than anything he'd felt for another woman before. His sudden, strong attraction to her was both exhilarating and unnerving.

And pointless, he reminded himself. Sierra was leaving soon, and despite the heat he sometimes imagined between them, she certainly hadn't shown much interest in him beyond that of a reporter in her subject. Maybe asking him to take her climbing had been an overture of friendship, or maybe it was simply more fodder for her story.

In any case, he wouldn't make a fool of himself by making the moves on a woman who wasn't interested. He'd take his cues from Sierra. She'd made no mention of wanting to see him today, so he'd stay away.

He laced on his hiking boots and pulled a day pack

from the closet, then whistled for Indy. With the dog running ahead, Paul climbed the steep trail behind his house and set out on the route that encircled the town. He set a fast pace, the rhythm of his strides and enginelike huff of his breath acting like a tranquilizer on his stressed nerves.

He pushed himself into a rough trot. The pack bounced uncomfortably on his back, but he didn't stop to adjust the straps. He wanted the discomfort, to take his mind off Sierra and the crazy emotions he wanted to outrun.

He alternately jogged and walked halfway around the trail, stopping only once to eat an energy bar. Three hours later, he descended and walked down into town. He'd have a beer at O'Brien's, then go home and take a shower, his head clear at last.

Indy drank from the dog bowl by the entrance to the pub, then found a shady spot to nap while Paul walked back to the patio. He froze in the doorway when he saw Sierra, sitting with Josh. It was as if he'd developed a homing instinct that always brought him back to her.

She laughed at something Josh said, the expression transforming her face, little lines crinkling at the corners of her eyes and dimples popping up on either side of her mouth. She looked so young and carefree when she laughed. He felt a sharp stab of jealousy that Josh was the one who'd made her look this way.

Then she looked up and saw him. Something bright

and joyous flashed in her eyes and his heart responded with a leap. She quickly masked the expression, and he might have told himself he'd imagined it, if not for the pink flush on her cheeks. Legs moving without conscious direction, he approached her table.

"Paul!" Josh looked up. "Where have you been hiding?"

"I took a run on the Perimeter Trail." Without waiting to be invited, he pulled out a chair and sat. Mandy, the waitress, came over and he ordered a beer. "What have you been doing?" he asked Sierra.

"Shopping," she said.

He glanced at the bags piled around her chair. The largest was from Ouray Mountain Sports. "What did you buy?"

"That's a secret," she said. The word itself, or maybe the sexy tone of voice in which she said it, made him feel too hot.

He took a long drink of the cold beer. "Sierra tells me the two of you are going to climb Uncompahgre Peak tomorrow," Josh said.

Paul nodded. "Are you ready?" he asked Sierra.

"I think I am," she said. "I hope so."

"The flowers should be spectacular this time of year," Josh said. "Just watch for signs of altitude sickness."

"I've felt fine since I got here," she said. "A little out of breath sometimes, but never sick. Should I be worried about tomorrow?"

"I doubt it." Paul shot Josh a look. *Thanks a lot for planting that worry in her head.*

"I shouldn't have said anything," Josh amended. "You'll be fine. People have the most trouble when they make a sudden ascent, like folks who fly in from sea level one day and go climbing the next."

"That's why mountaineers summit in stages, right?" she asked. "To give their bodies time to acclimate?"

"That's right," Paul said. "Though it's still a real strain to breathe, much less move, above twenty-two thousand feet. Your body feels like lead, and it's as if you're moving through quicksand. Every breath hurts and it's hard to think clearly."

"Your body is starving for oxygen," Josh said.

In this death zone, as it was known, there really wasn't enough oxygen to sustain life. Traveling there required extreme determination. The experience was always surreal, the mind clouded, the body slow to respond to the most basic commands. Mountaineers tried to spend as little time as possible in the death zone, but it was always one of the most challenging aspects of a climb.

"We won't be nearly that high tomorrow," Paul said. "We'll take it slow and you'll be fine."

She looked a little less confident, but nodded.

"Get a good night's sleep," he said. "We have to head out early in the morning."

"All right."

He was tempted to offer to come tuck her in—just to see her reaction. He might have done so, if Josh hadn't been there.

Sometimes he was sure she was every bit as attracted to him as he was to her. He wondered how far she would take things if he gave her the opportunity. Would she think it a lark to sleep with him, then leave at the end of the week, no more questions asked?

The problem was that he wanted more than sex from Sierra. She was a danger to his equilibrium because she made him think too much about the future—a future with her in it.

SIERRA KNOCKED on the door of Paul's house, but no one answered. She put her ear to the door and listened, but heard only the drumming of her own pulse in her ear.

She tried the door and it opened, revealing Paul, lying on his sofa. But this was Paul as she'd never seen him before—thin and drawn, and ghostly white. He stared at her with pain-filled eyes. "Sierra!" he gasped.

She rushed to his side and fell to her knees beside him. "Paul, what's wrong?" She stroked his forehead, which burned with fever.

"I'm sorry," he whispered, and closed his eyes.

"No!" she cried. She kissed his hot cheeks, and stroked his hair.

He wrapped his arms around her. "Don't leave me," he pleaded.

"I won't. I promise."

He opened his eyes again, his gaze searing her. "Come up here beside me," he said, and pulled her toward him.

She stretched out on the sofa next to him and he began to kiss the side of her neck, his tongue brushing lightly across the sensitive skin just below her ear, sending shivers down her spine. He feathered kisses along her jaw and across her cheek and eyes.

She took a sharp breath as his hand slipped beneath her shirt to fondle her breast. Whatever weakness had overtaken him before had fled, as if her presence had breathed life back into him...

Loud knocking on the door of her room jerked Sierra from sleep. She sat up, disoriented in the darkness, and clutched a pillow to her chest like a shield.

"It's just me," Paul said from the other side of the door.

Hearing his voice made her heart race harder; she'd been dreaming. He wasn't sick, and he hadn't been making love to her.

"Are you okay?" He sounded concerned now. "Say something."

"I'm fine," she called, and switched on the bedside lamp. The numbers 4:03 glowed in luminous red on the clock, like an angry brand. Did people really voluntarily get up at this insane hour? Apparently they did if they wanted to climb a mountain. "Just a minute." She stumbled into the bathroom, where she brushed her teeth and combed her hair.

When she emerged, the knocking had resumed. "You're going to wake up everyone on this floor," she said as she opened the door at last.

"The rooms around you are empty," he said. "Kelly mentioned it the other night." He moved past her. "Dress in layers. It's liable to be cold and windy up top."

"That's not what you told me yesterday," she said. "You went on about how beautiful it was."

"It's beautiful. But windy."

What else had he left out of his rapturous descriptions of the climb? But she said nothing—this climb was her idea and she wasn't about to back out because of a little wind.

She plaited her hair into a single braid, slathered on sunscreen and lip gloss and emerged from the bathroom once more.

Paul sat on the side of the unmade bed, bringing to mind once more her dream. She sat in the room's only chair and began to put on her hiking boots.

"Let me see your socks," he said.

"Excuse me?"

"You don't want to get blisters." Before she could protest further, he was on his knees in front of her, cupping her heel in one hand. The gesture was surprisingly intimate. His long fingers traced the curve of her instep, his head bent over her. She imagined she could feel his breath on her and hot arousal curled through her. She clutched the arms of the chair to keep from combing her fingers through his hair and pulling him to her.

"These cotton socks will end up giving you blisters," he said. His eyes met hers, dark with concern, but maybe with desire, too. Over his shoulder, the unmade bed beckoned. *Forget the hike,* she wanted to say. *Spend the day here with me, making love.*

But she couldn't make herself say the words. Professionalism or prudence—or that fear he'd accused her of earlier—kept her silent, and the moment passed.

He released her foot and stood. "I brought you some wool hiking socks." He fished a package from his pack and tossed it to her. "Try these."

"Thanks." She would never have thought she needed special *socks* for hiking up a mountain.

"Do you have a warm jacket?" he asked. "You'll need a pack, too. I have one in the Jeep you can borrow."

"I have my own, thank you." She proudly displayed the new hydration pack, which she'd filled with water the night before. "I have a fleece jacket, rain gear, a hat, energy bars and hiking poles, too." She didn't mention the first-aid kit, compass and emergency whistle the clerk at the outfitter's had sold her, afraid Paul would accuse her of overkill.

"You look all set," he said. "Do you have sunscreen?"

"Yes, Mother."

He laughed. "Hey, if we were in Manhattan, you'd

have to teach me how to get around on the subway and tell me the neighborhoods to avoid after dark."

"I guess so." Though Paul struck her as the kind of person who would educate himself about such things.

They gathered up her gear and she followed him downstairs and out to his Jeep. "Where's Indy?" she asked, surveying the empty backseat.

"Sleeping in." He started the vehicle and made a U-turn in the empty street. "He's done this climb before, but the rocks can be hard on the pads of his paws, and he doesn't like to wear booties."

So this "easy" trail was too difficult for his dog? She fought down a new wave of apprehension.

He handed her an insulated mug and a paper bag. "Breakfast," he said.

She started to tell him she wasn't hungry, but the aroma of coffee and breakfast burritos woke up her appetite. "Thanks," she said, and helped herself to the food. She began to feel more awake and more confident about the day ahead.

"Our timing is perfect," Paul said. "We should be on the trail for a beautiful sunrise."

His excitement was contagious; she began to feel the thrill of anticipation herself. "I can't believe you're this enthusiastic about a climb you told me you've done dozens of times," she said.

"I've never done it with you before," he said. "I can't wait to show you how beautiful it is."

She had to look away, afraid her emotions were

written too clearly on her face. He'd think she was pathetic, letting herself get so worked up over such a simple statement.

But the men she knew didn't share their lives this way. Their sports and hobbies and similar interests were kept behind a door labeled No Women Allowed. Not that Sierra wanted to care about basketball or sky-diving or new-wave punk bands, but it would have been nice to have the option.

But Paul wanted to share mountain climbing with her, and he was going to considerable trouble to do so.

After traversing a boulder-strewn four-wheel-drive road and crossing a shallow creek, he stopped the Jeep at a Forest Service trail head. "This is it," he said, shutting off the engine. "This is going to be great."

The flutter of excitement Sierra felt as she zipped up her jacket and shouldered her pack had little to do with the climb ahead. She was looking forward to a day spent with Paul in his element. For this one day, she'd try hard not to worry about the future or fret about the past.

CHAPTER EIGHT

THE TREK UP UNCOMPAHGRE Peak was one of Paul's favorites, past alpine meadows of jewel-like flowers opening onto expansive views of neighboring mountains and the valley below. There were other vistas as beautiful, from other mountains, but this was the only one he thought of as home. And today he had the chance to share it with Sierra.

She marched up the trail ahead of him, head up, shoulders back. He thought again of the first day he'd seen her, when she'd walked up his street in those impossibly high heels. From that very first glimpse of her, he'd looked at her differently than he had any other woman, admiring her strength and beauty, and wanting her for himself.

He wasn't entirely himself around her, but she made him want to be something even better—Paul 2.0, smarter, stronger, faster and more fun.

He moved up to walk alongside her where the trail widened. "This is Nelle Creek," he said, indicating the rushing stream that ran alongside the trail.

"What—or who—was Nelle?" she asked.

"I don't know. Maybe she was a miner's wife or daughter. But I do know Uncompahgre was the name of an Indian tribe that lived in this area."

"I wonder if they climbed the mountain," she said.

"I'm sure some of them climbed it," Paul said. "They would have wanted to see what was up there."

She glanced at him. "Is your motivation really that simple? To see what's up there?"

"Sometimes when I get to the top of a peak it's too foggy or snowy to see much of anything," he admitted. "Other times I see a lot of rock and ice and markers and flags left behind by others who have been there before me. There are very few major peaks that haven't been climbed by someone before."

"Then why bother, if you aren't the first?"

"Even if I'm not the first to climb a mountain, I'm still part of a pretty exclusive group. I like the physical challenge of doing something very few other people have done. There's a great sense of accomplishment in reaching the top."

"You could run marathons or enter long-distance bike races and say the same thing."

He shook his head. "It wouldn't be the same."

"You wouldn't be risking your life."

He made no reply. She wouldn't understand if he admitted that risking his life was an important part of what he did. He didn't have a death wish, but knowing one mistake or bit of bad luck could lead to his death reaffirmed how precious life really was. He liked being reminded of that.

They emerged from the trees into an open meadow and Sierra stopped and gasped. In the distance, gleaming silver in the early morning light, rose Uncompahgre Peak. It jutted above the plain like a jagged mastodon tooth, patches of snow flecking its granite surface. Sierra dug her new camera from her pack and snapped off half a dozen photographs. "I still can't believe we're going to climb that," she said.

"Wait until you see the view from the top."

They walked on, serenaded by the whistling of a fat marmot, who sunned himself on a boulder just long enough for Sierra to take a picture before he dived into his den.

Their pace was leisurely, much slower than Paul would have hiked on his own, but he didn't mind. Racing to the top was secondary to spending time with Sierra.

Two hours into the hike, as the grade increased, she began to breathe heavily. They stopped to allow her to catch her breath. "What elevation are we at?" she asked.

"About twelve thousand feet."

"If it's this hard to breathe here, how do people manage it at twenty thousand feet?"

"Stubbornness, I guess." He shrugged. "I just struggle through. Focus on the goal, or even just the next step. It's a mind game, believing you can succeed despite the physical struggle."

Her expression said she thought he was crazy, but she didn't waste her breath on the words. Instead she pulled out the camera again. "Let me take a picture of you and the mountain."

He posed with Uncompahgre rising in the background, then they set out once more. "Talk to me," she said as they trudged side by side. "Distract me."

"What do you want me to talk about?" he asked.

"What was the first mountain you climbed?" she asked.

"Long's Peak. You know that."

"I mean the first big mountain. Out of state."

"I did the tourist trip on Everest, but my first actual big summit was McKinley. Though its proper name is Denali now."

A shadow passed across her face, though she quickly composed herself, moving into journalist mode. "So your climb this spring wasn't your first time on McKinley?"

"No. I intended to retrace your father's route on my first trip." Ever since he'd sat as a teenager, glued to the television throughout the ordeal of Victor Winston's death, he had vowed to follow his idol's footsteps one day. "But the weather didn't cooperate that time, so I had to take a different approach," he continued. "This spring, I decided to try again."

And found his body. The words hung between them, unsaid. They'd both avoided the subject so far, and he was reluctant to bring up the unpleasant topic unless she asked.

"When I first heard you'd found him, I didn't believe it," she said. "When he died, it was really more like he'd just…vanished. Disappeared. I remember going to the memorial service and thinking that any moment he'd walk through the doors and explain there'd been a terrible mistake—that after the batteries in his radio died, he'd climbed down on his own, but had been too busy to tell anyone before. Not having a body in a coffin made it easier to believe those fantasies."

"I'm sorry," he said. "I never would have brought him down if I'd known it would hurt you."

"No, don't apologize. It's good to know for certain. Though of course I did know. No one could have survived that storm."

"Still, we never want to lose people we love. I think it's normal to hang on to any shred of hope as long as possible."

"I guess that's it. As long as he was still alive, I could hope that one day he'd want to be my dad again."

He opened his mouth to offer some trite bit of comfort—that he was sure her father had loved her, that of course she was special to him—then he shut it without saying a word. What did he really know about Victor Winston beyond the idealized image he'd built up in his mind? The man was a hero to him for all he'd overcome, but in climbing mountains and conquering new peaks, he'd left a bereft family behind.

Sierra turned away. "Are those clouds up ahead?"

He followed her gaze to a distant smudge of gray. "They're a long way off. Thunderstorms roll in a lot of afternoons, though, which is why it's a good idea to start early and be off the peak by noon."

They'd been hiking over three hours now. Sierra walked on with her head down, silent. He could hear the steady pant of her breathing. The grade increased, and he slowed their pace. He watched her closely. "Are you okay?" he asked.

"Let me just…stop and…catch my breath again." She walked a little off the trail and leaned against a boulder.

"Are you dizzy?" he asked. "Sick to your stomach? Do you have a headache?" He ticked off the symptoms of altitude sickness.

"A little bit of a headache maybe. But mainly it's just hard to breathe." She held up her hands. "My fingers are swollen."

"That's from walking with your hands gripping the trekking poles. They'll return to normal by tomorrow at the latest. Drink more water. That'll help your headache, too."

"My knees hurt, too. And my ankles."

"All normal." He took her hand and pulled her upright once more. "You'll feel better if you keep walking."

"What if I said I wanted to quit?"

Was she serious? "You're more than halfway there. You'll regret it if you don't go all the way to the top."

"Maybe you would, but I don't think I will."

"Don't quit," he said. It surprised him how much he wanted to get her to the top. He wanted her to experience just a little of what it was like to reach a summit—to know a little more about what he did, and about what her father had done. "You'll feel better at the top, I promise."

Still, she didn't move. "Haven't you ever wanted to quit?" she asked.

"Never."

"Not even when every part of you ached and you couldn't breathe and it was freezing cold and snowing?"

"I've aborted a climb because conditions made it unsafe," he said. "Unstable weather or avalanche danger or something like that. But I've never given up because of the physical discomfort."

"Why not?" Her eyes locked to his, trying to make sense of his stubbornness. "Why put yourself through all that?"

"To prove that I could," he said. "To prove I'm not a quitter."

"Prove to whom? Is someone keeping score?"

"To prove to myself, I guess." He looked away, frustrated that he couldn't make her understand. "That's part of what climbing is all about—pitting yourself against the environment. Testing yourself. Every time you suffer through hardship and make your goal, you come away a little bit stronger."

"How many times have you summited?" she asked.

"I've done all the seven summits—the highest peaks on each continent—at least once, some twice. There are fourteen peaks in the world over eight thousand meters in height, and I've climbed ten of them. I've done all fifty-four Colorado fourteeners, most multiple times, and I've climbed the fifteen California fourteeners and a bunch of lesser peaks. Why?"

"If you've done all that," she said. "Why not stop now, while you're still ahead?"

"Stopping means getting stagnant. Would you write one article, then quit?"

"That's different."

"I don't think so. Everyone likes new challenges. It keeps life from getting boring."

"It's also a good way to avoid other kinds of challenges." She shoved away from the rock and started hiking again.

He fell into step beside her. "What other challenges do you think I'm avoiding?" he asked.

She glanced at him. "How about relationships? Responsibilities. Obligations. You know—real life. Whenever something like that pops up, you can run away and climb another mountain."

"You're not talking about me now, are you?" he asked. "You're talking about your father."

"Maybe. I guess I'm trying to figure out how you're different from him."

"I don't have a wife or child or any other responsibilities that I'm running away from," he said.

"If you did, would you retire from mountaineering?"

"Why should I? There are plenty of climbers who have wives and families. They come with them on expeditions."

"Somehow I don't think being at base camp makes the waiting any easier," she said.

No, Sierra would not be one to wait at base camp, he thought. She wouldn't wait at all. His chest constricted, making breathing even more difficult. "I guess some women see supporting their spouse in his avocation as part of the commitment," he said.

"And some men obviously don't see how wrong it is to throw their lives away when they have a family," she said.

"There's a difference between taking calculated risks and being suicidal," he said.

"The end results aren't that different. And most women don't want to sit around waiting for those results."

"That's certainly true, but they might be missing out."

"Missing out on a lot of heartache."

This wasn't the woman who'd lost her father to a high-altitude blizzard talking, but the girl who'd seen her dad choose work over family. Victor might have done the same if he had been a pilot or a mechanic or a merchant seaman, but because he was a mountain climber, Sierra could never look on the profession as anything but destructive. Her view of Paul would always be colored by her distrust of his profession, no matter what other emotions he might stir in her.

He put a comforting hand on her back. "I can understand how you've had enough of that." He felt powerless to change that about her—after all, he couldn't go back and change her past.

PAUL'S HAND ON SIERRA'S back was warm and strong, in sharp contrast to the lack of feeling of which she'd accused him. How could she reconcile the man she was growing to like more and more with the reality of what he did for a living? How could repeatedly risking your life without considering how that risk affected your loved ones be anything but selfish and wrong? Yet she couldn't think of Paul as selfish when he'd been nothing but generous with her, giving his time as well as revealing so much of himself despite his initial reluctance.

Paul was smart, funny, handsome, sexy and thoughtful. He only possessed one real flaw—one that might indeed prove fatal.

"Do you ever think about doing something different with your life?" she asked.

"Not really. I like what I do, and I'm good at it."

"Yes, but do you plan to spend the rest of your life climbing mountains?"

"Sir Edmund Hillary was still climbing in his forties."

Another ten or fifteen years. "That's a long time to tempt death," she said.

"When you put it that way, yeah," he said. "But I don't think of it like that. At least not most of the time. I'm living my life in a way that never lets me take it for granted."

"There are some things I enjoy taking for granted," she said. "When I get up in the morning I take it for granted the lights will come on, that the coffee shop on the corner will have fresh coffee brewing, my desk will be the way I left it the night before and that I won't die before nightfall. It's a good way to live." She wanted a love she could take for granted, too—a man she could count on to be there for her every day.

"It would be nice to live that way," he said. "But I'm not sure that I could."

"Because it's not exciting enough?"

"I think it's more because I had to accept at a young age that I *could* die at any time," he said. "It's the kind of thing that stays with you."

His cancer. It was so easy to forget about that with him standing beside her so healthy. Was that really what drove him? "Paul, you're not going to die," she protested.

"Not anytime soon, I hope."

He stopped at the base of a rock spire. The view past him distracted Sierra from their debate. Struggling to catch her breath, she stared up at the steep slope filled with loose rock and boulders. "What do we do now?" she asked.

"There's a path to the left around the spire." He pointed to the narrow track. "It's a little exposed in places, but you'll do fine."

"Exposed? What do you mean by exposed?"

"There's a steep drop-off on one side, and you'll be walking pretty close to the edge. But don't worry."

She swallowed. "Did I mention I'm afraid of heights?"

"Really?"

"Not exactly, but then, I've never been up so high, out in the open before, either."

"Hold my hand. You'll be fine."

She started to refuse, then glanced at the narrow path again. No sense taking foolish chances. She shifted the strap of one trekking pole to her wrist, then slipped her hand into Paul's and allowed him to lead her around the spire and along the narrow path.

The trail was as wide as any city sidewalk, but bordered on one side by a wall of sheer granite and the other by a thousand-foot drop, it seemed as precarious as a balance beam. Sierra clung tightly to Paul as they inched across. She couldn't believe people actually did this for fun. Men like Paul and her father went out of their way to dance along the edge of disaster this way. Did they have some secret death wish, or was there something different in their makeup, some bit of DNA that made the danger not seem as real for them?

Pondering such questions held sheer terror at bay, though she didn't relax until they reached a wider expanse of rock that allowed them to move farther away from the edge.

"Take a look at the view," Paul commanded.

She forced her eyes from her feet and caught her breath. "You can see for miles," she said, gazing out at a patchwork of green meadows, wildflower-strewn tundra and snowfields below, all bound together by the silvery ribbon of the creek. It was like the view from an airplane, or rather, the view one might see standing on the wing of a plane, unobstructed by walls.

"It's even better at the top," he said.

By the time they reached the last stretch leading to the summit, she was able to let go of his hand and climb on her own. He led at a slow pace, turning often to make sure she was all right. His solicitude touched her. He was careful, but not condescending, and he seemed genuinely delighted to share this experience with her. She tried not to think about her pounding heart and aching chest as she struggled for each breath, or the leaden tiredness in her legs as she climbed the last few hundred yards. She was doing this, and she was proud that she hadn't given up. She'd made it to the top.

When she joined Paul at the summit, he stood at the very edge of the mountain. He pulled her up beside him, then put his arm around her, holding her securely as they gazed at what might have been the whole world spread at their feet.

"You did great." He looked at her, not the view, and she was conscious of her racing heart. It beat hard in her chest from a combination of exertion, thin air and maybe, also, from the presence of the man beside her.

"Paul, I...I never would have done this without you," she said. She'd never have seen the world from this vantage point, but she also wouldn't have made the effort to understand her father and resolve her feelings for him. Those feelings were still unsettled, but she'd made some progress. "Thank you."

"Thank you for letting me show you this." He continued to look into her eyes. Perhaps inspired by the risk she'd taken climbing this mountain, she rose on her toes and pressed her lips to his, her arms tight around him.

He tilted his head and deepened the kiss, sending a tremor through her. This was no tentative first kiss, but the embrace of two people who desperately wanted each other. Sierra felt a surge of triumph, knowing Paul returned her feelings. She felt giddy and reckless in his arms, emotions wholly unfamiliar yet exhilarating.

They were both breathless when he finally broke the kiss. They stared into each other's eyes, the view forgotten. "I've never gotten to do that at a summit before," Paul said. He brushed his thumb across her lips, smiling. "Nice."

Someone brushed past, mumbling "Excuse me," and Sierra looked away, suddenly self-conscious. At least half a dozen people had appeared on the summit from another path—all witnesses to that impulsive kiss. "What should we do now?" she asked.

"I can think of a few follow-ups to that kiss, but most of them are illegal in public. So let's sign the summit register," he said. Still holding tightly to her hand, he led her to a metal canister anchored to the mountain.

"Someone actually keeps records?" she asked.

"Sure." He unscrewed the end of the metal tube and took out a sheaf of paper and a pencil. "Not everyone bothers to sign, but most do, and now everyone will know that you were here."

She took the paper, and feeling only a little self-conscious, she wrote her name, the date and the time on the line provided. He signed just below her. "I should take your picture so you can show everyone back home," he said.

She handed over her camera and posed with a view of neighboring peaks stretched out behind and a little below her. "We should find someone to take one of us together," she said.

"Good idea." He turned and spotted a young couple crouched by the registry canister. "Will you take our picture?" he asked.

The couple obliged and Sierra and Paul stood arm in arm at the summit, smiling for the camera as the wind whipped Sierra's hair and tugged at their clothes.

"The wind is really picking up," Sierra said as she stowed the camera once more. "Those clouds look a lot closer, too," she said.

The dark mass, which only a few minutes before had seemed miles away, was racing toward them, smothering the sun and sending the temperature plummeting. She shivered and drew her fleece jacket more tightly around her.

She was about to ask him what he thought the temperature was when a distant lightning strike, followed by a boom of thunder, galvanized him into action. He counted the seconds between the lightning and the thunder out loud. "One-Mississippi, two-Mississippi… five-Mississippi." The storm was only five miles away, and moving fast. "We have to get down," he said.

Another jagged bolt of lightning tore across the sky, and a woman nearby screamed. Sierra grabbed Paul's arm. "Get me out of here," she said. Her father might have died on a mountainside, but she had no intention of doing so.

They clambered down the upper stretch of barren granite, following the handful of other people who had been on the summit when the storm first made its presence known. No one spoke, and soon the others were ahead. Sierra knew she was holding Paul back, but she couldn't make herself move any faster.

When they reached the narrow exposed trail, he took her hand to lead her across and she made no protest, gripping him so tightly her fingers ached.

They'd reached the rock spire when it began to hail, sharp ice pellets striking them like gravel thrown by some giant hand. The ground around them quickly grew slippery with ice. Her fingers dug into Paul's bicep as another loud clap of thunder sounded. "We should stop and find shelter," she said, looking around. "There might be a cave."

"No. We have to get off the mountain. All this bare rock is like a giant lightning rod."

As if to prove his point, another flash of lightning ripped through the air. Sierra tried to remember everything she'd read about death by lightning—something about open spaces like golf courses and, presumably, mountaintops, being the most dangerous locations in a thunderstorm.

They half ran, half slid down the loose talus slope. Sierra fell and sharp rock cut into her palms, but she scarcely noticed. She was too terrified to feel the aches and pangs that had plagued her earlier. If only she could move faster, or sprout wings and fly off this mountain. She'd never go near another one.

Next they had to cross a wide expanse of treeless tundra. It began to sleet, icy rain stinging like needles. Paul plowed forward, head down. Was he focusing on the goal of reaching the Jeep, or, as he'd said he did during difficult climbs, only on the next step?

She stumbled after him, thinking not of the next step but of her father. Had he ever been afraid—of lightning or avalanches or falling? Surely he'd been frightened at the end, when he'd known he was dying. Had he thought of her? Did he know she'd cried herself to sleep every night for a week, praying he would survive and come back to her?

These were the questions she'd ultimately hoped to answer with this trip to Ouray. This was the real reason she'd accepted Mark's assignment to interview Paul. But Paul himself had given her more questions than answers.

AT TREE LINE, the sleet turned to a steady curtain of rain. "Let's stop and put on our rain gear," Paul said, already unshouldering his pack.

"We're already soaked," she pointed out.

"It'll help some," he said.

She shrugged off her pack, head down, shoulders drooping. He cursed himself once more for getting her into such a predicament. "I should have paid closer attention to the weather," he said as he fastened his jacket. "I listened to reports this morning, but I ought to know by now how fast conditions can change at altitude."

Her rain suit crackled as she unfolded it from its pouch. The bright red vinyl stood out in the gray world, the way Sierra herself did. She didn't belong in his world, so why was he so determined to make her understand it?

She struggled to pull on the oversize raincoat and hood and he hurried to help her. "I think it goes this way." He twisted and turned the vinyl until it slid into place. Then he steadied her while she climbed into the pants. "There. That'll be a little better," he said.

She gave him such a classic look of skepticism he wanted to laugh, but he smothered the impulse. He wanted to kiss her again, but once he started, he wouldn't want to stop, and now was not the time or place. He helped her on with her pack. "You're doing great," he said. "The worst part is over. We're below tree line, so we should be out of danger."

She stared through the rain, up the path they'd just descended. He could no longer make out the summit of the mountain, shielded as it was by a silvery haze. "Was it as dangerous as it felt up there?" she asked.

"It could have been," he said. "Every year climbers are killed by lightning."

She shivered. "This is not something I have to deal with in Manhattan."

"Yeah, well, it was a great day until the weather turned on us," he said. He would never forget those few moments on the summit, their arms wrapped around each other, lips pressed together. He'd never shared a mountaintop with a woman before—having Sierra there made the moment so much more special.

But now she was wet, cold and exhausted. He'd be lucky if she ever spoke to him again after this. "Let's get out of here," she said, pushing past him and starting down the trail.

They reached the Jeep after two more hours of slogging through the steady downpour. They piled their wet gear in the backseat and Paul switched the heater to high, then turned to her. "I'm sorry," he said. "It was a beautiful day until the storm rolled in."

"You can't control the weather," she said, not looking at him.

"You'll feel better after a hot meal," he said. "Lake City has some good restaurants."

"I don't want to go to a restaurant. I want to go home."

By home did she mean Manhattan, or the Western Hotel? "We'll go back to my place," he said. "I have some dry things you can borrow."

"Do you have anything to drink?"

"Absolutely. We deserve a drink after the afternoon we've had." He began backing out of the parking area. "Dry clothes, hot food and a little alcohol will have you feeling better in no time." With a little luck, he could persuade her not to hate him for the rest of her life.

SIERRA STARED OUT the window of the Jeep, at the rain pouring in a silver curtain, turning the road into a river and blotting out the view of the mountains. She shivered, cold from more than the weather. She felt chilled to her soul.

Only a few hours before she'd been standing literally on the top of the world; it hardly seemed real now. Today had been a day of emotional heights and valleys, as well. Starting with that moment of intense longing in her hotel room, she'd gone from joy to despair and back again.

She was left feeling wrung-out and confused. Paul was the most amazing man she'd ever met: smart and sexy with a great sense of humor, kind and gentle yet strong. He had her thinking about things she hadn't allowed herself to contemplate before—love and commitment and happily ever after.

Yet he obviously wasn't considering anything like that. All he wanted to do was climb mountains for the rest of his life. What were the small satisfactions of everyday life on solid ground when he could ascend to great heights and look down on that life from above?

For all the ways he didn't resemble her father, the two men had one thing in common—that need to distance themselves from the people who loved them.

"You'll feel better once you're warm and dry," he repeated. She didn't really think he was reading her thoughts. Her misery was probably easy enough to diagnose from the way she was huddled in the seat, her expression glum.

"I'll feel better when I'm back in my apartment in Manhattan, with an order of Thai take-out, a good bottle of wine and decent shoes." When she was miles away from this man who had the ability to wound her without even realizing it.

CHAPTER NINE

PAUL PARKED THE JEEP in front of his house and began gathering the gear from the back. Sierra had thought about insisting he take her to the hotel, but then she decided he at least owed her a drink. And as much as she didn't feel like working now, there were still things she needed to know in order to complete her article.

She and Paul had both been avoiding the two-hundred-pound gorilla in the room—the events that had led up to him finding her father's body. Sierra had told herself she needed to gather all the information about Paul first, but really, she'd been putting off discussing a subject that was anything but pleasant. It must be upsetting to Paul, too, or else he was just very sensitive to her feelings.

Yes, he was a sensitive guy. That was one of the things that drew her to him. If Paul didn't exactly understand her, at least he tried. But she couldn't let her feelings about her father or Paul get in the way of writing this story.

Indy greeted them at the door with the enthusiasm of a dog who had been abandoned for days, overjoyed at this long-awaited reunion. Paul rubbed the dog behind the ears and fed him a biscuit, then went to work building a fire in the woodstove while Sierra pulled off her wet, muddy boots. "If you want, you can jump in the shower," he said over his shoulder to Sierra. "There's a robe on the hook on the door and I'll put some dry clothes in the bedroom for you."

She locked the bathroom door behind her, then left her soggy socks, jeans, shirt and underwear in a heap in the corner and stepped into the shower. As the hot blast hit her, she sighed and closed her eyes, letting the warmth seep into her.

With thawing came thoughts of how differently this day might have turned out. She and Paul might be sharing this shower now, the way they'd shared the experience of summiting the mountain. But the weather and her old fears had conspired against them.

She still wanted Paul's kisses, but they wouldn't come with a guarantee he wouldn't hurt her. The uncertainty paralyzed her.

She dried herself with a thick, fluffy towel, then slipped into the plush dark blue robe she found hanging on the bathroom door. The robe smelled like Paul, and she couldn't resist burying her nose in the sleeve and inhaling deeply. She stroked the soft fabric and wondered if the deprivations of his climbing expeditions had fostered an appreciation of luxury when he was home.

She found the clothes he'd promised, in a neat stack

on the end of his bed: sweatpants and a fleece shirt, and a pair of thick wool socks. The pants and shirt were too big, but she rolled up the legs and sleeves and snuggled into their soft warmth. She returned the robe to the bathroom and contemplated the pile of dirty clothes.

"I'll throw those in the washer," Paul said, and slipped past her to scoop them up. He'd changed out of his wet clothes into a pair of plaid flannel pajama pants and a long-sleeved T-shirt advertising a local brewpub.

"Make yourself comfortable by the fire," he said as he juggled the wet clothes. "I'll be with you in a minute with that drink."

The fire crackled in the woodstove, filling the room with warmth. Sierra sank onto the soft leather sofa and stared into the flames. She should insist on going back to her hotel room soon, but the warmth and comfort of the room combined with the exertion of the day had produced a pleasant lethargy she was loathe to relinquish.

"This should thaw you out." Paul came into the room, carrying two steaming mugs. He handed her one. It smelled of cinnamon and apples and something potent.

"What is it?" she asked.

"Apple cider, cranberry juice, cinnamon and rum."

She took a cautious sip. Sweet fire burned all the way to her stomach. "It's delicious."

"Do you want something to eat?" he asked. "I can't offer Thai take-out, but I can make sandwiches, or scramble some eggs."

"No, I'm fine." She sipped her drink and watched the flames dance in the woodstove, content despite all her earlier misgivings. This moment, right now, was perfect.

Paul sat on the opposite end of the sofa, his feet propped on the coffee table. "I never think these climbs tire me out until I stop," he said.

"Mmm," was all she could manage.

"How are your feet?" he asked.

"My feet?" Did he have some kind of fetish, always concerned about her feet?

"Did you get any blisters?"

"A couple," she admitted. They'd bothered her a little on the way up; on the way down she'd been too focused on getting out of the cold and wet to pay attention to a little pain in her feet.

"Let me see." He patted the sofa beside him and she swung her feet up to fill the empty space. With tantalizing delicacy, he pulled off one sock and then the other. Her skin tingled where he touched her, a sensation that traveled up her legs to settle at the juncture of her thighs.

He began to massage her foot, kneading the ball with his thumb, stroking firmly down her instep. It felt so amazing she wanted to moan. Then she realized she *had* moaned. She checked to see if he'd noticed. He was still focused on her feet. Gently he touched a blister. "I have some salve we can put on that later," he said.

Who cared about the blister? The man was driving her crazy with a foot massage. Her fatigue had vanished. She told herself she should pull her foot away, but she couldn't.

He transferred his attention to the other foot, then began to stroke her calf. If this was a clever way of getting into her pants, she had to admit it was working.

Having sex with Paul would be unprofessional and foolish and irresponsible.

It would also likely be wonderful, and no one would ever know but the two of them. She nudged Paul with her free foot. "You've started something now," she said.

His eyes met hers, the desire in them searing her. "What's that?"

"Now you're going to have to massage my whole body."

"I think I can manage that." He slid closer and leaned over her, his hand trailing up her leg, coming to rest between her thighs. She arched to his touch, another moan escaping her parted lips.

He cut off the sound by pressing his mouth to hers. He tasted of rum and apples, the sweep of his tongue in her mouth more intoxicating than any alcohol. He kissed her long and hard, while his hand continued to press her into the sofa.

She slid her hands beneath his shirt, over the ridged muscles of his abdomen and the sculpted contours of his chest. He pulled his shirt off and tossed it across the room, then returned to kissing her, his hands exploring beneath her shirt now, cupping her breasts in his palms, his thumbs flicking over her erect nipples. She was aware of his erection resting against her thigh, heavy and hot, blatant evidence of his need for her. She slid her hands beneath the elastic of his pants and grasped his buttocks, smiling at the firm perfection of him, pressing him down into her.

He paused once more to shed his pants, then helped her sit up and pulled her clothes off, as well. "Let's go into the bedroom," he said.

"I don't want to leave the fire."

"Then we'll bring the bedroom here." He climbed off of her and strode from the room. She turned to watch him, a giddy smile refusing to budge from her face as she contemplated his retreating backside and muscular thighs.

She took another sip of her still-warm drink and tried to banish the last flutter of apprehension as she contemplated sex with Paul. Her feelings for him were such a mix of fondness and fear, want and worry. The safest course would be to leave now, before things went any further. But if she didn't stay with him now, she knew she'd always regret it.

He returned with an armload of pillows and blankets and placed them by the fire. Indy trotted over to investigate. "Go to your bed," Paul ordered, and pointed toward the bedroom.

With a slow wag of his tail, the dog turned and left the room.

Paul stoked the fire, then Sierra joined him in arranging the bedding on the floor. "Mmm, comfortable," she said, reclining against a pile of pillows.

"Mmm is right," he said, angling himself over her. "Did you say something about a whole body massage?" He began stroking and kissing his way down her body, his hands and mouth caressing her breasts, stomach and thighs. Every nerve awakened to his touch, and she writhed beneath him, kneading his shoulders with her hands, crying out as his tongue flicked across her sex, almost bringing her to climax then and there.

Grinning, he raised his head, and groped in the tangled blankets until he found a square foil packet. She watched as he rolled on the condom, then she grabbed his arms and dragged him toward her. "I want you in me," she said. "Now."

"I like a woman who knows what she wants," he said, and pushed himself into her.

She wrapped her legs around his thighs and began to move. He matched the rhythm she set and soon they were both lost to the need building within them. She clung to him tightly, the way she'd grasped him at the top of the mountain. This time, when she hurtled over the edge, she intended to take him with her.

Of course, there was no pain or fear in this fall, just thrilling release and a warm, floating feeling. He tensed, then let out a long, low groan as he thrust hard into her.

She cradled his head on her shoulder and held him tightly when they were both spent, neither saying anything. There was no need for words now, not here in this warm sanctuary where, for this moment at least, neither the past nor the present could intrude.

SIERRA AWOKE TO DARKNESS and cold. The fire had gone out and the room and the world outside the windows were bathed in black. Her whole body felt stiff and her stomach growled with hunger. She sat and looked at the man sleeping beside her, a solid lump under the covers. Already their lovemaking was like a wonderful dream to her.

Why was life always like this, with real-world inconveniences and discomforts crowding out the fleeting, perfect moments?

Careful not to disturb Paul, she eased out from under the covers and over to the woodstove, where she attempted to rekindle the fire. The ashes were cold, and a brief search around the dimly lit confines of the hearth produced no matches.

She glanced back at their makeshift bed, but Paul slept blissfully on. She was *not* going to be the helpless female and wake him for something as simple as starting a fire. Shrugging into the robe, she went in search of matches.

The kitchen yielded nothing, though a curious Indy showed up to beg a dog treat. Sierra rewarded the dog for his efforts, and turned her attention to the hall closet. No matches here, either, though she did find a flashlight, which she used to search the rest of the shelves.

On the top shelf, the light illuminated a cardboard box, the kind used to ship reams of copy paper. Paul's name was scrawled on the side in a feminine hand.

"What are you doing?" Paul's voice sounded in the darkness. He moved over beside her. He was naked, his hair tousled, eyes drowsy-lidded. He looked sleepy and sexy and altogether tempting.

"I was cold so I was looking for matches to relight the fire," she said.

"Come back to bed," he said. "I'll take care of the fire." He started to close the closet door, but she put out a hand to stop him.

"Wait," she said. "What's in there?"

"In where?"

"In that box. The one with your name on it." She played the beam of light across the carton once more.

He frowned. "It's just a bunch of stuff my mom saved from when I was a kid."

"I want to see," she said.

He hesitated, and she couldn't help think of the irony—they'd just had sex, but looking at childhood mementos was too intimate?

"Okay." He lifted the box off the shelf and carried

it into the living room, where he set it on the coffee table/trunk. "Let me get the fire going and we'll take a look."

She returned to the relative warmth of the blankets while he switched on a lamp by the sofa, found his pajama pants on the floor and pulled them on. Within minutes he had a blaze roaring in the stove. He turned to Sierra. "I'm starved."

"Me, too."

"I'll see what I can find in the kitchen and we'll eat before we open the box."

While he was gone, she pulled on the shirt he'd loaned her, raked a hand through her hair and arranged the pillows so that she could lean back against the sofa. Paul returned with a tray. "I didn't feel like taking the time to cook," he said. He handed her a bottle of water and a pile of napkins and set the tray on the floor between them. Sandwiches, chips, a bunch of grapes and a bakery bag of cookies made for an impromptu picnic.

Everything tasted delicious. Sierra didn't know if it was the sex or the climb that had given her such an appetite, but it didn't really matter.

As they ate, she studied Paul out of the corner of her eye. His hair was mussed and the dark shadow of beard showed along his jaw. He hadn't bothered to put on his shirt, and the lamplight glowed golden on his skin, burnishing the taut muscle of his chest and arms.

She noticed a puckered scar on one side of his chest, just above his left nipple, and remembered

Kelly mentioning it. "What's the scar from?" she asked.

He glanced down at his chest. "Hickman catheter," he said. At her puzzled look, he explained. "It's a port they put in my chest to make it easier to draw blood and administer treatments. After I'd been sick for a while all my veins started collapsing and this made it easier. When I got well I had surgery to remove it, but it left a scar."

She felt a great tenderness for the boy he had been, and looked away, lest he mistake her feelings for sentimentality or pity. Maybe those things were part of the whirl of emotions he kindled in her. Whatever journalistic objectivity she'd had for him had long since vanished, replaced by a host of conflicting emotions. She desired him and yet wanted to distance herself from him. She hated what he did for a living, but was also fascinated by it. She admired his courage and strength while loathing his irresponsible attitude toward his future. She knew she was falling in love with him, and hated that he had made her so vulnerable.

"Why are you looking at me that way?" he asked.

"What way is that?"

"I don't know how to describe it. You look almost… angry."

"I'm not angry." Or if she was, it was with herself and her inability to make up her mind about him. She finished the last of her sandwich and reached for a cookie. "I want to see what's in the box."

"All right." He picked up the box and set it between them on the blankets, then lifted the lid. "My mom sent this to me after I moved into this house. I haven't looked through it in years."

She scooted closer. "This should be interesting."

"Either that, or really embarrassing." He took out the first item: a file folder of newspaper clippings. "Not too incriminating," he said, flipping through the yellowing newsprint. "It's a bunch of stories about my early climbs."

"She's obviously very proud of you," Sierra said, noting how each article was labeled in neat block printing with the date and the name of the mountain he had climbed.

He set the folder aside and reached for a scroll of paper fastened with a rubber band. Unrolling it, he grinned at the drawing of what looked like… "Mountains?" she asked.

"The Seven Summits," he said. "The highest peaks on each of the seven continents that a lot of professional mountaineers aspire to climb." He pointed to each peak in turn and named them: "Everest, Denali, Kilimanjaro, Aconcagua, Elbrus, Vinson Massif and Kosciuszko."

The mountains were each outlined in markers and decorated with the flags of their native country. A tiny Sherpa scaled the heights of Everest, while llamas grazed on the lower slopes of Aconcagua. "You must have spent hours on this," she said. "How old were you when you made it?"

"Fourteen."

"When you were sick."

He nodded. "I was going through chemo at the time and I started this as a kind of distraction."

"Did it help?"

"Some. Though I was only able to work in short spurts in between vomiting or sleeping."

He spoke so matter-of-factly, almost as if that horrible experience had happened to another person. "So even when you were in the hospital, you wanted to climb these peaks?" she asked.

"Wanted isn't really the right word. I was so sick, even going on a normal vacation or attending school, or simple things like that, seemed out of reach. The mountains were a fantasy, one that helped me forget about the real world for a while."

"But you didn't forget about them when you were well. You went and climbed all these mountains."

"I did." He rolled up the poster once more and lifted out a hiking-boot box. "Here's something you'll want to see," he said. "The Victor Winston archives." He handed her the box. "Go ahead. Open it."

She flipped back the lid and stared at the collection of newspaper clippings, books and videos—all about her father. She unfolded a yellowed newspaper clipping that told of Victor's solo ascent of K2. "My mother used to have a box of things like this," she said. "But I haven't seen it in years."

"You're welcome to take it back to the hotel and look through it."

"Thanks." She wasn't ready to read through a recap of her father's life with Paul watching. She set the box aside and he delved into the carton once more.

He pulled out a sheaf of hospital bracelets, bundled together with a rubber band and fanned out like a crazy white-and-gray pom-pom. "Oh my gosh." She fingered the end of one bracelet. "Are all these yours?"

"Yeah. Pretty pathetic, huh?"

She reached past him and snagged a red-and-black bandanna. "Did you wear this?" she asked.

"After I lost my hair, yeah."

She studied his thick brown hair. "I can't imagine you bald."

"Hopefully it's something you'll never see." He tugged the bandanna from her grasp and tossed it back into the box, then replaced the lid. "I should throw this out," he said.

"No!" She put her hand on his.

"Why not? It's just a bunch of junk."

"You should keep it to remind you of what you've been through. Of how far you've come."

"It's not something I'm likely to forget." He shoved the box out of the way. "Mainly, I don't like to think about my cancer. It's something I went through, but it's not important to me now." He nodded to the boot box and file folder. "You're welcome to keep those as long as you like. Maybe you'll learn something interesting."

She frowned at the yellowed clippings slipping from the folder. "I don't want to read old articles about you, or about my father." She drew her knees to her chest and wrapped her arms around them. "I want you to tell me about him. About finding his body."

He looked at her, eyes filled with concern. "Are you sure?"

No. She could never be sure. But she'd come all this way to learn the truth. She didn't want to put it off any longer. "I want you to tell me everything," she said. "I want to know what it was like up there where he died."

PAUL HAD KNOWN THIS MOMENT was coming, though he'd wanted to put it off as long as possible. He hated the thought of causing Sierra a single moment's pain, but then again, maybe the pain had been inflicted long ago. Maybe telling what he knew would somehow help her heal.

He leaned back against the sofa and began as he'd been told to begin all stories, at the beginning.

"I told you Victor Winston was my idol, so I followed his career the way some kids follow baseball players or race-car drivers. I read everything I could find about him and I even had a map where I marked all the peaks he'd summited."

"You really were a geek," she said, almost smiling.

He nodded. "I was pathetic. Anyway, when it was announced that he was going to make a solo climb of McKinley, on a new route that had never been climbed before, I was excited about it. I searched the papers every day for reports of his progress."

"You were what—sixteen then?"

He nodded. "That's right."

"What were you like?" she asked. "What was your life like?"

He'd been a skinny kid with a geeky obsession none of his classmates shared. He'd been through an ordeal they couldn't begin to understand and all those things made him an outsider. "It had been two years since my bone-marrow transplant," he said. "My hair had grown back and I'd started lifting weights, trying to catch up with my classmates, who hadn't spent two years in and out of the hospital." He'd had friends, but always felt a bit separate from them, like someone from another country trying to fit it with the natives. Maybe it was because he couldn't share their teenage sense of invulnerability. His battle with death had shown him how precarious life could be.

"I bet you were cute," Sierra said.

"No. I was definitely a late bloomer." He cringed at the memory of his awkwardness.

He knew what she would have been like: she'd have been the beautiful girl he wanted so badly to notice him—the smart, confident, almost magical creature who didn't even know he was alive. She would have been the girl he could never have, so he'd have convinced himself there was no sense even wanting her. Such perverse logic had worked when he was sixteen, but he had no hope of fooling himself that way now.

"So you followed my father's expedition to McKinley." She brought them back to the subject at hand.

"Yes. I gave a report for social studies about your father's proposed climb, and three days later the story broke that he was stranded on the mountain in a blizzard."

The way he remembered it, the whole world had been focused on the battle to try to save the lone climber. "I listened to all the television reports. I thought it was so amazing that even though his life was in danger, your father continued to radio updates. Even when the news was grim, he sounded so strong and positive." The way Paul wanted to be.

"My mother and I listened to those reports, too," Sierra said. "I was fourteen and I still remember how unreal it felt. My father was huddled in a sleeping bag on the side of a mountain in a blizzard, yet in those dispatches he sounded almost like he did when he called to wish me a happy birthday. I even thought for a while it might be some kind of publicity stunt."

"But it wasn't," Paul said.

"No. It wasn't. But still, I could hardly believe it was happening to him—to my father."

"That last day, when the dispatches ended and the weather worsened, was wrenching," Paul said. "It must have been a hundred times worse for you."

She rested her chin on her knees and stared across the room, though he had a feeling she wasn't seeing his plastered walls or heavy curtains. "I was so afraid for him," she said. "My thoughts just kept alternating between hoping he was alive and imagining him dying alone up there. But mostly, I was angry."

"I've always heard anger is part of grief."

"Why was he even up there?" she asked. "It seemed like such a waste."

"He was doing what he loved," Paul said. "Is that ever a waste?"

"Yes. In this case, I think it was. But tell me how you ended up finding his body. I never understood why the search parties that went up after the storm cleared couldn't find him."

"Part of the difficulty was that your father had kept parts of his route secret, afraid someone else might beat him as the first to climb that part of McKinley," Paul said. "And there was speculation that when the weather turned nasty he may have gotten off course and not been in the location where he told rescuers he was."

"Why was he up there by himself?" she asked. "Doesn't that make it that much more dangerous?"

"He wanted to do a solo climb—something no one had done in that area before. It's something climbers do, always challenging themselves, setting new goals."

"Were you looking for his body?" she asked. "Did you think you might find it?"

"I knew it was a possibility, but I never thought it would really happen. I assumed he had been buried by an avalanche or swept into a crevasse years ago."

"But he hadn't."

"No." He fell silent, gathering his thoughts, trying to find the right words. "I don't know what made me look in that direction, but I had a feeling—call it an instinct or hunch or whatever—that something wasn't right about what I was seeing, so I hiked over to take a look."

It had been a precarious location, on a steep slope, and he'd told himself he was being foolish to veer off course that way, but he was drawn to the area as if by a magnet.

"I saw the sleeping bag first," he said. "It had faded a lot, but I could still see a bit of the blue. Then I saw the…the hand sticking out of it." It had looked like a leather glove, dried and withered as a mummy by the arid, cold temperatures. It clutched at the faded blue cloth, the glove that had once covered it in shreds around the wrist.

"Did you know it was my father?" Sierra asked. "I mean, I guess you weren't expecting anyone else up there…"

"He wore a watch. His name was engraved on the back." He'd hesitated to examine the body, but told himself he had to be sure. He had never felt more alone than in that moment, the only sounds that of the wind and his own harsh breathing. He had the eerie feeling of being close to death, as if Victor had expired only moments ago, instead of more than a decade before.

"Why did you decide to bring the body down?" she asked. "It must have made your climb much more difficult and dangerous. You could have used GPS to mark the spot for rescuers to retrieve later. Or you could have left him where he was. No one would have known."

"I'd have known." He shook his head. "Maybe it was foolish, but I couldn't bear to leave him alone again after all this time." Carrying the body, still wrapped in the sleeping bag, had been awkward, but it was lighter than he'd expected and he'd felt humbled by the task of doing something for the man who had inspired him for so many years.

He glanced at Sierra, trying to read the emotions in her face. "Are you sorry I recovered his body?" he asked. "Would it have been better for you if you hadn't had to go through burying him and mourning him all over again?"

"Easier maybe, but not better." She sighed. "I've lived my whole life with the feeling that there was unfinished business between us."

"I suppose it often feels like that when someone we're close to dies unexpectedly," Paul said.

"That's part of the problem. We weren't close, though. Not the way we had been. After he and my mother split up, I didn't see him that often. He could have seen me anytime he'd wanted. My mother wouldn't have stopped him. But he was always away on an expedition or filming a television show or scouting a new location. He didn't have time for me anymore."

The thing that had saved Paul's life had stolen her father from her. "That must have been hard," he said. Lame words that offered little comfort, but he could think of nothing else to say.

"I resented him for never saying goodbye," she said. "He could have sent word to me and my mom—instead he chose to speak to the media. But he must have known we were listening."

"Maybe he didn't want to upset you."

"As if watching him die on television wasn't worse?"

Her voice didn't waver, and her eyes were dry, but he heard the pain in her words, and felt her suffering as keenly as if it was his own.

"Come here," he said, and held out his arms.

She came to him, and he did his best to comfort her, the only way he knew. Kisses and caresses turned to lovemaking. Paul wanted to protect Sierra. To be with her now, and maybe forever. But what did he have to offer her but more pain?

She'd asked if he'd consider doing something else with his life besides climbing. But what?

The truth was, he was afraid. Afraid that if he stopped challenging himself, stopped pushing his limits, stopped fighting to stay aware of the gift of life every minute, then death, which should have overtaken him years ago, would finally catch up.

CHAPTER TEN

IF THEIR FIRST LOVEMAKING had been the wild, inevitable collision of two bodies drawn together by a powerful attraction, their second coupling was gentler and more intense—the union of two souls who needed each other.

Sierra sensed the difference. After years of grieving alone for her father, Paul had mourned with her, and in doing so, had taken some of her pain away.

He lay beside her now, sleeping, half out of the covers, mouth open, snoring softly. She didn't consider it a good sign that she found this absolutely adorable.

She lay on her back again and stared at the ceiling as the first pale streaks of sun stretched across the white plaster. What had she gotten herself into? She wasn't like this—she didn't have sex with men she'd been assigned to write about. She didn't have sex with men she'd only known a few days. She didn't have sex with men she'd never see again after this week.

She'd thrown out all the rules when it came to Paul. Such freedom was exhilarating—and very scary.

"Hey, beautiful." He stirred, then snuggled close, one arm draped across her stomach. He kissed her neck, sending a current of awareness down her body. His hand slid up to cradle her breast and she moved away.

"I can't believe how sore I am this morning," she said.

His grin was positively wicked. "I'd say I was sorry, but I hate to lie," he said.

Her face burned. "I'm sore from the *climb*," she said. "Not from anything else."

"I know just the cure for that. You need a soak in the hot springs." He threw off the covers and stood.

"I need a what?"

"A soak in the hot springs." He pulled her up beside him. "It'll loosen up those stiff muscles and have you feeling better in no time. Did you bring a swimsuit?"

She kept her eyes on his face, trying to ignore the fact that they were both naked. "Yes. It's back at my hotel." As if that wasn't perfectly obvious.

"We'll stop there on the way. I'll take a quick shower, then we can go." He slid his hands to her hips. "Care to join me?"

She pulled away. "I don't think so. I'll just, um, straighten up in here."

"Suit yourself." Whistling, he sauntered toward the bathroom.

As soon as he was out of sight, Sierra snatched up her clothes and began dressing. Paul had the power to make her forget herself. She'd never felt so *vulnerable* with a man before.

Having her clothes back on helped, as did venturing into his kitchen and raiding the refrigerator for breakfast. Not that being waited on hand and foot hadn't been nice, but she was a woman who was used to looking after herself and she needed to stay in practice. If Paul decided to whip up a gourmet brunch it might weaken her resolve even further.

Coffee and food would help clear her head and settle her shaky nerves. She'd take advantage of these moments alone to remind herself who she was—and who Paul was—and all the reasons why there was no future for them together.

PAUL DIDN'T CLAIM to be an expert on women, but it didn't take a Casanova to see that something was bothering Sierra this morning. He emerged from the shower wide-awake and ready for a repeat of the previous night's great sex and found her dressed and seated at his kitchen table, a notebook, file folders, index cards and pens arranged in front of her like land mines set out to thwart an enemy. One of the file folders from the carton his mother had sent was open in front of her. Standing in the doorway clad only in a towel, he felt decidedly underdressed and unwelcome.

"Let me fix you some breakfast," he offered.

"No, thank you," she said, not even glancing up from her notebook. "I already helped myself."

"Finding anything interesting?" he asked, nodding at the file folder. On closer inspection, he saw it was the one that contained articles about his early climbs.

"A little," she said, not looking up.

Maybe it was from his years of hanging out with Sherpas, but he knew when to keep his mouth shut, so he retreated to his bedroom, dressed and grabbed his bathing suit. "The hot springs are going to feel great," he said when he returned to the kitchen. "Let's go."

Silently she packed up all the papers and they drove to the Western Hotel. This was a dangerous moment; Paul expected her to announce she'd changed her mind about coming with him to the pools, but maybe her sore muscles won out over any sudden objections she had to him. "I'll be down in a minute," she said.

Paul went in search of coffee and found Kelly on duty in the dining room. "You're looking grumpy this morning," she said.

He ignored the comment. "Can you get me a cup of coffee and a breakfast burrito?" he asked.

"Sure." She gave him a curious look, and retreated to the kitchen.

He leaned back against the old wooden bar, and watched the stairs. Maybe he should have gone up to Sierra's room with her. Alone up there, she might decide to ditch him.

Kelly returned with a steaming mug of coffee. "I thought you'd be in a better mood this morning," she said. "Word is Sierra hasn't been back to her room since early yesterday—when she left with you."

He sipped the coffee and said nothing.

Kelly put her hands on her hips. "Well? Do we need to send out a search party, or is she still with you?"

"She was with me. Right now she's up in her room, getting her bathing suit so we can go to the hot springs."

"Then why do you look so glum?"

He studied Kelly, considering his options. For all her faults—she was vain, self-centered and single-minded in her determination to be an actress—she was also sweet, kind and levelheaded. And she was a woman, who might have some insight into what another woman was thinking. "Everything was going great," he said. "We spent the day and the night together and had a terrific time. Then I woke up this morning and she won't touch me, doesn't want me to touch her. She hardly looks at me. She's not unfriendly, but she's not exactly friendly, either."

"If you want to know what's going on with her, you should ask her," Kelly said.

If he asked her and she confirmed his worst fears—that she didn't want anything more to do with him—what then? At least by avoiding the issue he could still be with her.

"I thought maybe she was upset about her father," he said. "I told her about finding his body last night."

Kelly made a face. "Aren't you the romantic guy. What kind of pillow talk is that?"

"She wanted to know."

"I guess it's not all bad. You're the hero who brought his body back so it could be buried properly."

"She's not treating me like a hero."

"Oh, cheer up. She agreed to go to the hot springs with you, didn't she? Maybe she's just not a morning person."

Paul glanced toward the stairs. "She's taking an awfully long time. Maybe she changed her mind."

"Or maybe she decided to take a shower and put on some makeup. She wants to look gorgeous for her lover boy." Kelly smirked. "I'll be back in a minute with that burrito and some more coffee. You need to keep your strength up for later."

Maybe Kelly was right and he was making too much of this. Any minute now, Sierra would come down those stairs and everything would be fine.

But if she didn't, he'd go up after her. He hadn't waited this long for a woman he could love only to let her get away so easily.

SIERRA DEPOSITED her notebook and files on the desk next to her laptop, then dug her bathing suit from her suitcase. She debated taking another shower, but settled for changing clothes and brushing her hair. The longer she stayed in this room, the easier it would be to hide here from Paul for the rest of her stay.

That was the coward's way out, and she definitely wasn't a coward. Whatever she was feeling for Paul, it obviously wasn't love. Love was a pleasant emotion. Euphoric, even. People crossed continents, risked their safety, even turned their backs on everything they knew for the sake of love, so it couldn't be like this.

Being with Paul made her confused and angry and even afraid. She couldn't think straight when she was with him, and the sooner she got away from him, the better off she'd be.

But the thought of leaving him made her want to cry—and she never cried. It also made her want to scream, and she wasn't much of a screamer, either. She was tempted to call the airport and change her reservations so that she could leave today and pretend that none of this had ever happened.

But running away wouldn't help her figure out why Paul made her feel this way. And it certainly wouldn't get her article written. If her father could conquer remote, dangerous mountains year after year, she could face down one smiling mountain climber and live to tell the tale.

Downstairs, she found Paul leaning against the bar, eating the most enormous breakfast burrito she'd ever seen. While she'd been so nervous and upset this morning she'd barely been able to eat a piece of toast, his appetite obviously hadn't suffered at all. The sight of him devouring the burrito annoyed her. Why did he have to be such a…such a *guy?*

"I'm ready to go," she said.

"*Gmmmph.*" He nodded and shoved the last of the burrito into his mouth and followed it up with a gulp of coffee. "Okay," he said.

He sauntered past her to the front door, the picture of a man without a care in the world. She was dying inside, but he didn't even notice. A man who had feelings for her—a man who loved her—would notice, wouldn't he?

He held the door for her and she marched past, eyes forward, determined not to betray her feelings. Last night had been beautiful and tender, but obviously those feelings had passed. She and Paul would never be a couple and she'd been crazy to entertain the idea for even a moment. All she had to do now was get through the next two days without letting him know she'd been so delusional.

MIST HUNG IN A GAUZY VEIL over the water of Ouray Hot Springs, obscuring vision and muffling sound so that people spoke and moved as if in a dream. Paul eased into the pool, exhaling as the hot water enveloped him. He settled on a ledge and waited for Sierra.

He'd been ready to climb the stairs to her room and demand an explanation for the long delay—and for her sudden coolness toward him—when she'd finally descended the stairs. She'd had nothing to say until he'd parked the Jeep in the parking lot of the hot springs and they'd agreed to meet in the pool outside the bathhouse.

He'd been tempted to ask her to confide in him and tell him what was wrong, but he'd kept his emotions in check and played it cool. If she had anything to say to him, he'd wait her out. He believed in the old saying that it was better to keep his mouth shut and be thought a fool than to speak up and remove all doubt.

A smudge of red caught his attention. He tensed as Sierra emerged from the mist, a red bikini hugging her curves, her hair piled loosely atop her head. She spotted him and waved, her expression solemn, then lowered herself into the pool.

"This water is hot," she said when she reached his side.

"A hundred and six degrees. We can move to a cooler part of the pool if you like."

"No, it feels good." She lowered herself to the ledge beside him and sighed. "It feels wonderful. I've never been anywhere like this."

"Uncompahgre, the peak we climbed yesterday, is the Ute word for hot-water springs," he said. "It's what they called this whole area. The Utes were coming here to soak in the springs a long time before white men even knew they existed."

"It's a pretty incredible place," she said.

You're an incredible person, and you make me feel incredible things. But he couldn't say the words out loud. Not yet.

She closed her eyes and he could feel the tension

leave her, and he began to relax, too. Maybe now, while they were both more at ease, was a good time to clear the air between them. "I know some of what I had to say last night was hard for you to hear," he said. "Are you okay with that? Do you have any more questions—about your dad and what happened?"

"None that you can answer."

He imagined some of those unanswerable questions: Why did Victor Winston leave his family? Why did he have to die, alone on that mountain?

He put a hand on her shoulder and squeezed gently. "I'm sorry," he said.

Her eyes snapped open. "You didn't hurt me," she said. "My father is the one responsible, but it all happened a long time ago. There's no sense continuing to rehash it now."

He may not have been the direct cause of her pain, but by bringing Victor's body down off that mountain, he'd opened the wound again. He regretted her suffering and his part in it. But better to change the subject.

"How's the story coming?" They'd covered a lot of ground in the interviews, but had she learned all she wanted to know about him?

"I think it's going well. I may write a sidebar about our climb yesterday—the famous mountaineer's daughter conquers her first peak."

"You did great," he said. "I don't know if I told you that." *You* are *great*.

"Thanks. It was a good feeling, getting to the top."

"Then you understand a little of the thrill of reaching a high summit."

"I'll never understand why someone would risk his life to do such a thing," she said.

No, she wouldn't. Only someone infected with the mountaineering bug would. "I guess some of us are driven to take such risks," he said. "Whether that's positive or negative is a matter of perspective. From my point of view, you take a bigger risk living in a big city like New York."

She laughed. "I'm not going to fall off a cliff or freeze to death in Manhattan."

"No, but you could be run over by a taxi, or killed by a human predator." He sank lower in the water, letting the soothing heat flow over his shoulders. "We all have different ideas of what poses a threat," he said. "I'm not deliberately courting death up there on the mountain. I know the risks and try to prepare for them."

"Where is my notebook when I need it?"

"I'll repeat the quote for you anytime you like." But her comment stung him. Did she only see him as the subject of her interview? As an assignment, a job? After last night, did she still not think of him as a man? One who cared for her very much?

She trailed her hands through the water. "Tell me more about the springs," she said.

"Are you thinking of putting them in your article?"

"Maybe. Or maybe I'll write a travel piece about the wonders of Ouray."

"The town and the county are named after Chief Ouray, the Ute chief who signed the treaty that signed over the San Juans to white settlers. This pool area was built in the twenties."

"I can see why the town wanted to capitalize on such a resource."

"There's another hot springs over toward Ridgway, and undeveloped springs along the river. There are some fabulous trails I'd love to show you, and you haven't even seen Silverton yet, or the narrow gauge train." He had so much he wanted to share with her.

"I never realized there would be so much to see and do in such a small place," she said.

"You should think about staying here for a while. Maybe use up some vacation. Or…" He hesitated.

"Or what?"

He wished the mist didn't obscure her expression. Was she open to what he was suggesting at all, or did she think he was nuts? "I'd like it if you stayed longer," he said.

"I have a job," she said. "An apartment."

Details. His heart lifted. She hadn't said no. "You're a writer. Writers can work anywhere. And I'll bet even in this economy, apartments in Manhattan are in demand. You could sublet your place."

"And live in the Western Hotel? No, thank you."

"You could move in with me."

There. He'd said it. This was as close as he could bring himself to begging her not to go.

He'd heard of loud silence before and had never known what the expression meant, but now, it became all too clear. His ears rang with the silent shouts of the voice in his head that screamed at him to take the words back.

"You're not serious," she said at last.

"Why not? We get along great together." On the surface, maybe asking her to move in with him was a rash suggestion, but doing so had given him the same giddy rush he got summiting a mountain—the same hyperaware feeling of being alive.

"We hardly know each other."

"You know more about me than any other person alive, and after last night, I think I know you pretty well, too."

"No. It's a crazy idea. I can't believe you'd even ask me." She moved toward the ladder, as if she intended to leave.

"Wait!" He took her by the wrist, holding her back. "I want to get to know you better, and I can't do that if you go back to New York."

"Planes fly in both directions, you know. Why don't you come to Manhattan?"

He swallowed hard. "Is that an invitation?"

Their gazes locked. He held his breath, hoping the look in his eyes would be enough to sway her.

She turned away. "No, it's not an invitation. Things would never work out for us."

"How can you say that? We're good together." She made him feel better than he had in years. He didn't want that good feeling to stop. "You make me think about something besides climbing. No one has ever done that for me before."

"That's what you say now, but it wouldn't last."

He released her. "Then you won't stay."

"I can't. And you can't come with me. We'd only make each other miserable."

"Because I remind you of your father? I'm not him. I won't hurt you that way."

"Yes, you will. You won't mean to, maybe, but one day you'll go off to Katmandu or Tanzania or Alaska and you won't come back. I might as well fall for a man with a mistress. I'd still have to share him, but at least he'd have a better chance of staying alive."

"Don't leave, Sierra." Now he *was* begging. Damn pride, anyway. "You're the only woman I can see myself being happy with," he said.

"And when I look at you, all I see is the past repeating itself." She climbed out of the pool and walked away through the mist, never even looking back.

SIERRA TUGGED JEANS and a shirt over her still-wet body and hurried from the bathhouse, praying Paul wouldn't follow her. She didn't want to make a scene on the streets of his hometown; they'd both be better off if he let her slip away quietly. She'd send him a copy of her article when it was done, along with a polite but impersonal thank-you note, and they could both pretend last night had never happened.

So much for thinking she'd inherited any of her father's courage.

Apparently, he hadn't passed on much of his stamina, either. By the time she completed the long hike back to the hotel, she was huffing and puffing and every muscle in her body was protesting. She dragged herself up the stairs to her room. Hadn't these people heard of elevators?

The neatly made bed tempted her, but she resisted the urge to crawl under the covers. She could sleep the day away and maybe when she woke she'd find this had all been a dream.

But that only happened in bad television shows. Staying in town—even long enough for a nap—would only make her problems worse.

She hauled her suitcase from the closet and began stuffing clothing into it, not bothering to separate dirty from clean. She was on her knees by the bed, reaching for a discarded sock, when a knock on the door made her freeze. She didn't want to talk to Paul, didn't want to listen to him try to persuade her to stay.

The knock sounded again. If she pretended she wasn't here, would he go away?

"Sierra, can I come in?" Kelly called.

Aching muscles protesting, Sierra shoved to her

feet and went to the door. A check of the peephole showed Kelly standing by herself in the hallway, fidgeting impatiently.

Sierra opened the door. "What is it?" she asked.

"I really need to talk to you," Kelly said, and slipped past Sierra into the room. She sat on the edge of the bed, ignoring Sierra's suitcase. "I may have done something really stupid," she said.

"What is that?" Sierra asked. She really didn't have time to listen to Kelly, but she didn't want to be rude to her, either.

"I went out with Keith last night, to a really nice restaurant in Telluride." She lifted her chin and tucked her hair behind one ear in an imitation of her usual bravado, but her trembling fingers and pale cheeks betrayed her real distress.

Sierra sat next to her. "What happened?" she asked. Had Keith refused to finance her New York trip?

"It was an amazing evening," Kelly said. "He…he told me again how much he loved me—that I was the most special woman he'd ever met. And he asked me to marry him."

Sierra had trouble breathing, remembering the moment when Paul had asked her to move in with him. Not as romantic as a marriage proposal, but every bit as potentially life-changing and unexpected. "What did you say?" she asked. Hearing how Kelly had handled this situation might help her to deal with Paul.

Kelly looked at her, the younger woman's dark

eyes shining with an emotion Sierra couldn't interpret. "I told him yes," she whispered.

"Yes?" Sierra pressed her hand—still holding the sock she'd fished from beneath the bed—to her chest. "What about New York? What about your acting career?"

"I know it's crazy," Kelly said. "But when he asked me, the yes just popped out. He told me he loved me and wanted to be with me forever, and I couldn't bear to leave him. No one has ever loved me like that before."

"Do you love him?" Sierra asked.

Kelly nodded. "I do," she said. "I really do." She covered her face with her hands. "What am I going to do?"

"Marriage is a big step," Sierra said. "You shouldn't go through with it unless you're absolutely sure." Where had that come from? She sounded like someone's mother, though she was only a few years older than Kelly.

"I know." Kelly sighed. "I've spent years planning my escape to New York. It's what I've always wanted."

"Then you should go. You shouldn't let a man stop you."

"Yes, but…I really do love him. And leaving him to follow a dream that might not even come true doesn't seem so great anymore."

"Then maybe he could go with you," Sierra said. Though trying to pursue an acting career and handle the demands of a new marriage sounded pretty tough to her; it wasn't the exciting, carefree adventure Kelly had no doubt dreamed of.

"He might do it," Kelly said. "But he has a good business here, and a nice home and…well, I love it here, too."

"Before, you talked like you couldn't wait to leave."

"Yes, but…I guess when someone you love is in a place, it helps you see that place in a better light. It really is beautiful here, and I have so many friends. I don't know anyone in New York."

"You'd know *me*." Small comfort, probably. "And you'll meet new people, make new friends. New York is beautiful, too, in its own way." She couldn't believe the driven, ambitious young woman she'd first met in this room was willing to toss all her dreams away for the sake of a ring on her finger.

"What will all those new people matter if I'm missing Keith? I've never felt this way about anyone before. What if this is my one chance for true love and I throw it away?"

All the advice she'd ever heard about love filled Sierra's thoughts: if he really loves you, he'll wait for you. If you found love once, you'll find it again. Love that demands sacrifice isn't real love.

But was any of that advice true? What did she know about building lasting relationships? Her parents' marriage had ended when she was only ten, and she'd never been involved in a serious relationship herself.

If anything, she'd done everything she could to avoid losing her heart to a man. She'd told herself she was better off living life on her own terms, free from anyone else's demands. But when she thought of a future spent alone, she felt empty and a little scared. Was that what Kelly was feeling now, too?

"If you stay here with Keith, don't you think you'll eventually regret not going to New York and trying to make it as an actress?" Sierra asked.

Kelly plucked at an artfully frayed spot on her jeans. "We talked about that, a little. There are a lot of regional and community theaters. I could audition for more roles in Telluride and Lake City and even Grand Junction. That would be a good way to build a reputation and credits. From there I might move on to Denver. I could pursue my dream and still stay close to home."

It made good sense. But what was sensible about changing your whole life for the sake of a man?

"You should give yourself more time to think about this," Sierra said. "You don't want to rush into anything."

Kelly nodded. "You're right. I mean, it's not like we have to get married tomorrow. And New York will still be there next week or next month or next year if I change my mind." Her smile turned dreamy. "And Keith will be there, too. That's a great thought, you know? That he'll be there for me the rest of my life."

Sierra felt sick. How could Kelly be so sure Keith

would be there for her? Sierra's mother had counted on Victor Winston to be there for her, and he'd left to climb mountains instead. Then again, Keith was a real-estate developer—not a profession that was particularly dangerous or bordering on obsession. Oh, why couldn't Sierra have fallen for a real-estate agent, or a plumber, instead of a damn mountain climber?

"Thanks for listening," Kelly said. "I think just talking to someone has really helped me. I got a little panicky this morning when I woke up and realized what I'd done. It's a big decision, you know."

Sierra nodded. She'd experienced the same kind of panic when she woke this morning next to Paul. Too bad talking with Kelly hadn't clarified things for her any.

Kelly shifted on the bed, bumping into Sierra's open suitcase. "Hey!" she said. "Are you packing? I thought you weren't leaving until Monday."

"Yeah, well, I decided to see if I could get an earlier flight back to New York." If not, she could always get a hotel room and spend the night in Montrose.

"Why? Did something happen with you and Paul? Did you have a fight?"

Sierra shook her head. "It's just not going to work for us. I need to get home."

"But Paul's crazy about you—crazier than I've ever seen him about any woman. I think he's really in love."

"He asked me to move in with him."

"Wow. That's pretty sudden, isn't it?"

"Exactly. I've only known him a week! He can't expect me to change my whole life for him—especially when he knows how I feel about what he does for a living."

Kelly looked thoughtful. "Mountain climbing does take him away a lot."

"Mountain climbing will get him killed!"

"Oh. Yeah. I guess you'd know about that." Kelly patted Sierra's knee. "I'm sorry. Paul really is a great guy."

"He is. But a relationship with him would be wrong on so many levels."

"I guess I'm lucky. Real-estate agents tend to stay put and they don't risk their lives." She stood. "Is there anything I can do for you before you go?"

"No. But thanks for offering."

"Take care." Kelly's expression brightened. "And who knows—I may see you in New York after all. I'm thinking it would make a great destination for a honeymoon."

When Kelly was gone, Sierra sank onto the bed. She was still holding the sock—one of the pair of hiking socks Paul had bought for her. He'd been worried she'd get blisters. She'd never met a man who was so thoughtful. So kind and brave. The kind of man it would be easy to fall in love with.

But whatever she was feeling for him, it obviously wasn't really love. She wasn't dreamy-eyed like Kelly, and New York didn't look any less attractive to her because Paul wasn't there. She couldn't wait to return to familiar surroundings, where she could think clearly and get back to the life that had seemed perfect before Paul had tried to make her think differently.

CHAPTER ELEVEN

PAUL WAS STILL SITTING at the pool, too stunned by Sierra's departure to move, when Kelly raced in. "What are you doing, just sitting there?" she demanded.

"What?" He blinked at her. "Is something wrong?"

"Sierra's leaving."

"No, she's not. Her flight isn't until Monday."

"She's packing her suitcase and going now." Kelly crouched at the edge of the pool, her sandals showing red-polished toes even with Paul's chin. "Did the two of you have a fight?"

"We didn't fight." Not really. Neither of them had raised their voices or spoken in anger. Sierra had been upset and walked away, but he'd assumed she was merely going to cool off. "Did you say she's packing?" His brain was having a hard time working, as if he was in the death zone, deprived of oxygen.

"She's leaving right now, unless you do something to stop her."

The image of Sierra walking out of his life forever was enough to get him moving. He climbed out of the pool and, not bothering to find his shoes or even a towel, raced to his Jeep and headed toward the hotel.

Two blocks from the pool, he passed a white sedan headed in the opposite direction. He had a fleeting impression of dark hair framing a beautiful face, then the vehicle was past him.

She was really leaving. How could she really be leaving? He whipped into a U-turn in the middle of Main Street, ignoring the blaring horn of a braking truck and the glares from pedestrians, and raced after the rental car.

Honking his horn, he drew alongside Sierra. She stared at him. "Stop!" he shouted.

She shook her head and sped up, but he increased his speed, as well. He had to stop her here, on this straight stretch of road before they entered the canyon. "This is ridiculous!" he shouted. "Stop!"

She pulled over at the entrance to the ball fields and got out of her car as he reached her. "Are you crazy?" she demanded. "Were you trying to cause a wreck?"

"Don't go," he said. "Whatever I did to upset you, I'm sorry."

She stared at him. "You don't know why I'm so upset?"

He shook his head. "We were talking about your staying in Ouray and I offered you a place to stay—"

"You asked me to move in with you."

"Well, yeah, but—"

"You asked me to move in with you when we'd only known each other five days."

"I wanted us to be together." Was that so bad?

"We had one wonderful night together and you expected me to leave my life in New York and come live with you in little Ouray, Colorado, and do what—wait patiently while you gallivant all over the world to climb mountains?"

He winced. Was that how it had sounded to her? "I wasn't thinking. I just…things were so good between us, I didn't want it to end."

Her expression softened, some of the anger going out of her eyes. "I can't stay here," she said.

"Not even until Monday?" Even a few more days would be better than this sudden, unexpected departure.

"There's no point."

"Not even if I tell you I love you?"

The words hung between them. He held his breath, and wondered if she was holding hers, too. Her cheeks paled, then flushed, and she let out a rush of air. "It's not enough," she said softly.

In every love song he'd ever heard, love was supposed to be all you needed. How could it not be enough? "What would it take for me to change your mind?" he asked.

She didn't hesitate to give her answer. "You'd have to quit risking your life climbing mountains. And it wouldn't be right for me to ask that."

Any more than it was right for him to ask her to abandon her life for his sake. What did other people do in situations like this? They found a middle ground—compromised. Something he'd had little practice at. "I love you," he said again.

"It would be very easy for me to fall in love with you," she said. "But it would be the wrong thing for both of us." She opened her car door. "I left those files with Kelly at the hotel. You can pick them up anytime."

He didn't want the damn files. He wanted her. But when you'd told a woman you loved her and she was determined to leave anyway, what else could you possibly say? "I never met anyone like you," he said.

"You'll always be special to me, Paul." She leaned forward and kissed his cheek, then slid into the driver's seat and drove away.

He stared after her, forcing back the mix of rage and pain that washed over him, trying to make sense of what had just happened.

Was he crazy to think he could love a woman he'd known such a short time? But Sierra had been a part of his life for so much longer. She was the baby in the sling carried by Victor Winston up the mountain in the video he'd watched a hundred times. She was the person Victor smiled at in the picture Paul kept. She was the grieving daughter Paul had thought of as he carried Victor's body down the mountain.

She was the woman he'd been waiting for all these years. If only she'd been waiting for him.

PAUL CONQUERED MOUNTAINS by thinking of only one step at a time. Sierra thought of that advice often as she struggled through the next few days, then weeks. This was her life, and this was what she had to do. The pain she felt wasn't as physical as a mountain climber's suffering, but it was just as crippling. Ironically, writing about her father and about Paul had gotten her through the worst of it. She settled back into her job and into life in New York as if nothing had ever happened, though inside, she felt she'd never be the same.

"Terrific job on your article. Our readers are going to love it." Mark beamed across his desk at Sierra the day after she'd turned in the piece. She'd been back in New York two weeks now—Ouray, Colorado, might have been a dream.

"Thanks." She couldn't say she'd enjoyed writing the profile of Paul—parts of it had been emotionally wrenching. But she was proud of her work on the piece.

"I appreciate that you made the article so personal," Mark continued. "I especially liked the part where you wrote about how your feelings for your father changed as you learned more about his death. That's the kind of insight no other journalist could have brought to this piece."

She'd written that hearing Paul's story had helped her understand why her father sought out the heights of the world—because he wasn't capable of handling the emotions and complications of everyday life. Mountains were simple. They required strength and stamina and a fierce concentration on the task at hand. On a mountaintop, the problems of real life seemed far away and small. As long as a person stayed on the mountain, those problems remained remote and insignificant. "I hope this pays off for you," she told Mark.

"It already has." His grin broadened. "I'm heading up a special quarterly supplement focusing on endurance sports. And it came with a nice raise."

"Then you definitely owe me dinner."

"You name the date—though I hope you don't mind if Tabitha comes along. She knows about our romantic history and I think it would make her uncomfortable if we went out to dinner at an expensive, romantic place, no matter how innocent our intentions."

"Not at all. I should probably get to know your future wife better. And I can dish all the dirt on you."

Mark looked worried for a moment, but he quickly realized she was teasing. "That's great. And I was thinking—Tabitha has a brother who's single. I could invite him along."

"Thanks, but I'm not interested." She still felt too wounded and vulnerable to date anyone so soon after Paul.

"He's a really nice guy. I think you'd like him."

"No, really. Not now." She offered what she hoped was a cheerful smile. "I don't want a new guy to watch me make a pig of myself at your expense."

Mark laughed. "Okay. Well, check your calendar and let me know when you're available."

She left his office and took the elevator down to *Cherché*'s headquarters. As she stepped into the hall-way, she met her editor, Cassandra Evans, a tiny woman with an imposing presence. "Love those shoes," she said, zeroing in on Sierra's red Louboutin heels.

"Thank you," Sierra said, with a pang of sadness. The shoes made her think of Kelly, which in turn reminded her of Paul. In the two weeks since she'd left Ouray, seldom an hour went by that she didn't miss him. She'd told herself that the feelings would lessen once she completed the article, but so far that hadn't proved true.

"I'm putting together the winter calendar," Cassandra said. "What ideas do you have?"

"I want to do something on children's cancer—maybe an article about the female doctors and nurses who care for the kids." The image of Paul as a sick little boy—all those hospital bracelets!—had stayed with her.

Cassandra looked thoughtful. "It's not sexy or glamorous, but if you focus on these women as facing real challenges, accomplishing great things…" She nodded. "I think our readers would like it. Give me an outline by the end of the week."

Back in Sierra's office, a courier had left a package. She read the return address—Ouray, Colorado—and a wave of dizziness swept over her. So many times in the past weeks she'd thought about the town, and the people she'd met there. She'd imagined what life would have been like if she'd accepted Paul's offer and stayed—but of course, that was impossible.

She backed carefully to the door and shut it, then sat at her desk and stared at the padded envelope. What could Paul possibly be sending her?

Or was it from Kelly? The idea both disappointed and relieved her. She found a pair of scissors in her desk and cut open the envelope.

Inside was something small wrapped in bubble wrap, and a letter in a slim white envelope. She picked up the little package and turned it over and over in her hand. It was about the size of a tangerine, and felt hard beneath the wrapping.

When she unwound the protective layers, she stared at the red jade figure of a dragon—a netsuke.

Her throat tightened as she stared at the little figure. It was just like the one her father had given her for her tenth birthday, right before her parents split. But how had Paul known?

She opened the envelope and unfolded the letter:

Dear Sierra,

I meant to give this to you when you were here, but the opportunity never presented itself. I'm sure you recognize it as a netsuke. Your father had it with him when he died. I probably should have sent it to your mother with the rest of his effects, but I wanted something of my hero for myself.

I realize now that was wrong, and I apologize for keeping this. I'm sure it will mean much more to you than to me.

I feel I owe you another apology, as well. In my happiness over the amazing night we spent together, I got carried away, but I had no right to pressure you to change your whole life based on that one night. I admire and respect you too much to think you would be so rash. Please believe this—you are an amazing woman and you will always be special to me.

I can't help but think that your father kept this little dragon with him as a reminder of you. He may not have visited as often as he should have, but you were in his thoughts, even in his last moments.
All my best,
Paul

She blinked rapidly, her eyes stinging. The jade warmed in her hand as she clutched the netsuke to her cheek. She thought of her father, alone on that mountain in a blizzard, knowing the end was near. He'd been thinking of her. He *did* love her, even if he didn't always know how to show it. That knowledge was the greatest gift anyone could have given her—worth more than diamonds or gold, or even the antique jade netsuke.

She would treasure the little dragon, though, as tangible evidence of the ties that bound her to her father.

She'd think of Paul when she looked at the dragon, as well. He'd apologized for his impulsive invitation, but she owed him an apology, as well. She'd been a coward, running out of town as she had, and she was big enough to admit her mistake.

She pulled a blank piece of paper from the printer tray and found a pen, then stared at the smooth white sheet, wondering how to begin. She couldn't remember the last time she'd written a personal letter. It was such a quaint, old-fashioned way to communicate. Didn't Paul have e-mail?

But she was a writer, she reminded herself. She made her living finding the right words to say. So she picked up the pen and began:

Dear Paul...

PAUL HAD HEARD ABOUT heartache in a thousand books and movies but he'd never known it was a real, physical thing until now. The pain of missing Sierra was almost constant these days, as if the old wound from the Hickman catheter had become infected.

He knew that to endure great suffering, one had to find a way to distract the mind until the pain passed. Focusing intently on other things had gotten him through grueling cancer treatments and up torturous mountain slopes. The pain didn't hurt any less, but concentrating on other things helped him hang on until the agony eased.

He took out his maps and atlas and began planning a new climbing expedition. He charted routes, made lists of supplies, drafted itineraries and inventoried his equipment. He would focus on what he knew, and forbid himself to think about what might have been. Getting through this was like climbing a mountain— you lived one moment at a time.

He had his climbing ropes and harness stretched across the front yard one morning when Josh found him. "Hey, Paul," Josh said. "You're just the man I'm looking for."

"Oh? Why is that?"

"You hear the news about Kelly?"

"What news?" Kelly had avoided him since Sierra had left town, apparently miffed at Paul for not doing more to stop her. But how could he stop a woman who had clearly made up her mind?

"She eloped."

"Eloped? With Keith?"

"Yeah. Is that crazy or what?"

"It's a little sudden, but it's not so crazy if they love each other."

"But Kelly—married?" Josh shook his head. "I thought she was all set on going to New York and becoming a famous actress."

"I guess she changed her mind."

"I've heard women do that, though none of them ever changed their mind about me."

Paul nodded. And Sierra wasn't likely to change her mind about him, either. He'd sent that letter, hoping she'd reply and they could at least be friends, but so far she'd remained silent.

"You busy right now?" Josh asked.

"Not really. Why?" If Josh wanted to go for a climb, Paul was up for it, as long as his friend didn't ask too many questions.

"Another group of kids from Children's Hospital are coming in next week. We could really use another volunteer to help with their climb over at the pool wall."

"No thanks. That's really not my thing."

"Oh, come on. It's better than sitting around moping."

"I don't want to, okay?" he snapped.

The same relentlessness that made Josh a good partner on a climb made him insufferably annoying at times like this. "Why not?" he asked. "These kids have cancer—they're not contagious or anything. They've been through a tough time and we're trying to give them and their families a vacation they'll never forget. And you won't give up one afternoon to help?"

"It's not that—look, I had cancer when I was a kid."

"You did?" Some of the anger eased from Josh's expression. "And you never said anything, all the time I've known you?"

"It's not something I like to talk about."

"Then you should definitely help these kids. Seeing you, grown up and healthy, would be a real inspiration to them and their families."

"I don't like being reminded of it."

"Why not? You're over it. Time to move on."

"I have moved on." Moving on meant not dwelling on the past. Just last week he'd dumped the whole carton of stuff from his mom in the Dumpster. He didn't need those reminders of what had happened to him.

"Be that way, then," Josh said. "But if you change your mind, we're meeting the kids at ten Thursday morning over at the pool."

Paul waited until Josh got in his truck and drove off before he rolled up his gear and stashed it on the porch. Then he headed into town to the post office, a ritual he'd performed every day at this time for a week, ever since he'd sent the letter and netsuke to Sierra.

The thin stack of mail in his box raised his hopes,

and he anxiously rifled through it. He discovered a phone bill, two credit-card solicitations, a sale flyer from an outfitter in Montrose and, at the very bottom of the pile, a slim envelope with a New York postmark.

With trembling fingers, he tore open the envelope and pulled out a single sheet of paper covered in a neat, feminine sprawl:

Dear Paul,
Thank you for the netsuke. Having it means so much to me, but the words you sent with it are an even greater gift than the object itself. I know you meant for them to comfort me, and they did.

I left without telling you how much your kindness and friendship meant to me. You made a difficult situation less difficult and in spite of the way things ended, I wanted you to know that.

The truth is, the strength of my feelings for you frightened me. I felt I had to put some distance between us, to gain some perspective. Now, two thousand miles away, I know that I fell in love with you. Under different circumstances, you might have been the man I stayed with forever.

But we are who we are, and forever isn't possible for us. We can't remain lovers, but I hope we will be friends. When you are alone on a mountaintop somewhere at the far reaches of the world, I hope you will think of me.
All the best,
Sierra

He folded the letter and slid it back into its envelope, then stared at the New York postmark. Sierra had admitted on paper that she loved him, though she thought it was impossible for them to be together.

Her words made him feel the way he had when he'd been accepted to his first expedition to Everest: elated, overwhelmed and just plain scared. She loved him. But she didn't love what he did. The profession he'd chosen made it impossible for them to be together.

She'd told him what he needed to do to be with her. He had to give up the only thing he knew—the profession he not only loved, but the thing that defined his life, that defined *him*. If he quit climbing mountains, what would he have left?

What had he really accomplished in all his years of climbing? It was a question he'd avoided looking at too closely. What did it matter what his achievements meant if he was doing something he was good at and it made his life better?

But he couldn't say climbing improved his life now, when it kept him from the woman he loved. So what was he trying to prove? That he was still alive? That he could cheat death again? That if he did enough great things, he deserved to survive what others had not?

But had he done enough to deserve the love of a woman like Sierra—a woman who knew better than most what a harsh mistress the mountains could be?

"AND THEY ALL LIVED happily ever after—but Danny was happiest of all." Sierra closed the book and smiled at the little boy who sat beside her. He wore a camouflage bandana around his bald head and had a temporary tattoo of a lightning bolt on his left forearm. His name was Tom, but Sierra called him Tough Tommy. He was eight years old, and battling a cancer with a name she didn't even try to pronounce. "How did you like that story?" she asked.

"It was pretty good," Tommy said. "I liked the part with the pirates best."

"I'll see if I can find another book about pirates for our next visit," Sierra said. She stood and helped the little boy crawl back under the covers. "You look really good today," she said.

"I had a transfusion yesterday, so my hemoglobin count is really good." He spoke with all the nonchalance another boy his age might have used to talk about video-game statistics or baseball scores.

"The doctor thinks he might be well enough to go home in time for his birthday next week." An attractive blonde—Tommy's mother—spoke from the doorway.

"Your birthday!" Sierra said. "What day?"

"September 15." Tommy grinned. "I'm asking for a dirt bike."

"He's determined to turn all my hairs gray," his mother said. She came over and put her hand on her son's shoulder. "My little daredevil."

"Mo-om!" Tommy rolled his eyes.

Sierra laughed, and said goodbye to them both. *I'll have to find something special for Tommy's birthday,* she thought as she left the hospital and headed down the sidewalk toward the subway. She hoped his high spirits today indicated he'd turned the corner, and that he would live to see many more birthdays.

Then, as they did often these days, her thoughts turned to Paul, another daredevil cancer survivor. What was he doing as fall came to the mountains? He hadn't answered her letter yet, but then, it was probably too soon.

She checked her watch. She had enough time to grab a salad at the deli on the first floor before returning to her office to work on her article about female doctors and nurses at the forefront of children's cancer care. Researching the article had led her to volunteer with St. Jude's Hospital, and to her friendship with Tommy.

The receptionist waylaid her in the lobby of *Cherché.* "There's a couple in the waiting room who asked to see you," she said. "They told me they were friends of yours."

Curious, Sierra left her salad with the receptionist and hurried to the waiting room. When she opened the door, she was startled to see Kelly and Keith. "Sierra!" the younger woman exclaimed, and threw her arms around her.

"This is a surprise!" Sierra returned the hug, then

stepped back to survey the couple. Keith wore nice slacks and a pale Oxford shirt with the sleeves rolled back to reveal an expensive watch. Kelly was dressed more flamboyantly, in black leggings, spike heels and a Puccini-inspired tunic. Half a dozen bracelets jangled on her wrist, and she carried an oversize designer bag. Anyone spotting her on the sidewalk would have pegged her as a model or actress—definitely not a waitress from a small town in Colorado. "What brings you to the city?" Sierra asked.

"We're on our honeymoon!" Kelly displayed a diamond-encrusted band alongside the large solitaire on her ring finger. "We eloped three days ago."

"You eloped? Congratulations!" The announcement left Sierra a little breathless. She glanced at Keith. His gaze was fixed on Kelly, as if he couldn't bear to tear his eyes away for even a second. Was that kind of devotion worth changing one's whole life plan? She shifted her attention back to Kelly, who looked jubilant. "Will you be in New York long?"

"Only two more days," Kelly said. "I have to get home in time to begin rehearsals for the Creede Repertory Theater's Christmas Show."

"A show? So you'll be acting locally?"

"Yes!" Kelly could barely contain her glee. "It's a very respected regional theater. And I've already been asked to try out for a dinner theater in Grand Junction."

"She's an amazing talent," Keith said. "They're lucky to have her."

"Sounds like everything is going great," Sierra said.

"Better than I ever imagined," Kelly said. She looked at Keith. "We're seeing a lot of shows while we're in town, and as much as I'd like to be on Broadway, I'm really happy where I am now."

"That's great. I'm glad to hear it," Sierra said.

"Have you heard from Paul?" Kelly asked.

Sierra fingered the netsuke attached to her purse. "We've exchanged a couple of letters," she said. It wasn't enough, not compared to the closeness they'd shared in Ouray. She still remembered how it had felt to look through the collection of items from his childhood and see the life he'd lived—she'd felt connected to him through their mutual love of her father. But that same connection—the very thing that had destroyed her father's relationships and eventually ended his life—made it impossible for Paul and Sierra to ever really be together.

More than once, she'd told herself she never should have written to him. That it would have been better for both of them to make a clean break. But she hadn't been able to banish him from her life. No matter how much he frustrated her, she cared about Paul, and wanted to know how he was doing.

"I'm glad you're in touch," Kelly said. "You two were good together."

On paper, Sierra had been able to admit she loved him—as crazy as that was, after less than a week with him. Maybe the propensity to fall so hard and fast ran in families. Her mother swore to love her father forever after only knowing him a week, and as far as Sierra could tell, Jennifer had kept that promise.

So maybe Sierra loved Paul, but that didn't change anything about their circumstances.

"So what have you been up to?" Kelly asked.

"I've been volunteering at Children's Hospital. I read to the kids, or play games, keep them company and give their parents a break."

"That must be heartbreaking—all those sick children."

"It is—and it isn't. They're really terrific kids, and seeing them cope with their illness makes my own problems seem pretty small." Volunteering with the children had helped her feel closer to Paul, too. She felt she understood him a little better now. Maybe his wanting to climb mountains wasn't so different from Tommy wanting a dirt bike for his birthday, though shouldn't a grown man—even one who had suffered a grave illness—be past such things?

"Honey, don't forget your appointment at one-thirty," Keith said.

"I'm getting my hair done at a very exclusive salon," Kelly said. "I had to beg them to work me in but they finally agreed."

"Kelly can be very persuasive," Keith said, grinning.

"Have a wonderful time in the city," Sierra said. "Congratulations, again."

They parted at the lobby entrance. As Sierra turned back toward her office, the happiness she'd carried with her from the hospital faded, replaced by wistfulness. She envied Kelly and Keith their happiness. A few months ago, she'd rarely thought about marriage and children. She hadn't been sure she wanted either in her life.

Maybe confronting her feelings about her father had changed her ideas about family and being a parent. Or maybe being with Paul had showed her a glimpse of what it would be like to share her life with a caring man. Ever since she'd returned from her visit to Ouray, she'd been able to picture herself as a wife and mother. She understood now why Kelly had exchanged her dreams of Broadway stardom for a very different kind of life. Love really did have the power to transform the way a woman looked at the world.

Kelly had taken a chance on love and hit the jackpot. In playing it safe, Sierra couldn't decide if she'd saved herself a huge heartache, or guaranteed she'd regret her decision forever.

CHAPTER TWELVE

THURSDAY MORNING, Paul knocked on Josh's door a little after nine o'clock. "Hey, what's up?" Josh asked.

"If I agreed to help you with these kids this morning, what would I have to do?" Paul asked.

"Just help spot them on the course. Answer questions, encourage them a little. Nothing tough."

"How sick are they?"

"I don't know." Josh scratched his chin. "I mean, they've all got some kind of chronic illness that keeps them at the hospital, but they're well enough to make the trip."

Paul thought of a trip to Disney World he'd taken shortly before his transplant. He hadn't wanted to go, but one of those organizations devoted to fulfilling the last wishes of dying children had given his family the trip and his parents hadn't wanted to turn them down.

At fourteen, Paul thought he was too old for Disney. People stared at his bald head and skinny frame, and the rides made him vomit. When a guy dressed up like Mickey Mouse tried to get him to pose for a souvenir photo, Paul threatened to punch him. His father got mad, his mother cried and they went home a day early.

He wanted to believe no camping expedition for these kids could be as bad as that, but what if it could? "I'll try to help," he said. "But if it gets too heavy, I'm leaving."

"Just look at it like a tough mountain—grit your teeth and keep working your way to the top."

The two friends rode to the pool in Josh's truck, loaded with climbing gear. Paul was grateful for Josh's silence on the short drive; some people would have asked him how he was feeling, or wanted to know more about his cancer—neither subjects Paul cared to talk about.

Two vans full of kids and their parents were unloading in the parking lot when he and Josh arrived. At first glance, the children looked like any other group of boys and girls, ranging in age from six or seven up to midteens. They wore shorts, T-shirts, tennis shoes and ball caps and some carried backpacks.

But closer inspection revealed balding heads under the ball caps. Some had the puffy "moon" faces indicative of steroid treatments, while others were unnaturally thin and pale. Had he really ever been so young and vulnerable?

The camp leader, a stout woman named Veronica who was relentlessly cheerful, introduced Josh, Paul and a few other local volunteers. "These guys are going to show you how to climb safely and have a lot of fun," Veronica said. "And when we're done here, we'll all head to the pool."

Cheers went up at the mention of the pool, then everyone lined up to be fitted with climbing harnesses and helmets while parents took pictures.

Paul spotted a teenage boy off to the side, arms folded across his narrow chest, expression sullen. "Are you with the group?" Paul asked.

"What clued you in, Sherlock? Was it the bald head, or the needle tracks?" He thrust out his thin arms, which were crisscrossed with scars. Paul's own arms itched, remembering the sensation of having no veins left that didn't roll or collapse, but knowing the nurses would be in again soon to try once more to find some new place to stick their needles.

"What's your name?" he asked. "I'm Paul."

"Rocco."

"Do you want to climb, Rocco?" Paul asked.

Rocco folded his arms again and scowled at the rock face. "Why would I want to do that?"

"To prove to yourself you can."

"I don't need to prove anything. You just want to get your jollies helping the poor sick kid. Go help someone else. I don't need your pity." He glared at Paul, but behind the insolence and anger Paul recognized the fear—not the fear of rocks or falling or even of making a fool of himself, but the cold terror he himself had lived with for too many years—the fear that had made it tough to close his eyes at night, in case he never woke up again. The fear that the illness he battled was too big, and just might win.

"What do you think people see when they look at you?" Paul asked.

Rocco shrugged. "What do I care?"

"Do you think they see the bald head, the skinny frame and think 'oh that poor sick boy'?" He delivered the words with a saccharine whine. "Is that what you think?"

Again the shrug. "Some of them probably do."

"Is that what you see when you look in the mirror."

"I don't look in the mirror."

Paul felt his heart contract. Oh, yeah. He knew exactly where this kid was at. Had been there, so disgusted with his own reflection he'd covered the bathroom mirror with a towel. He leaned closer and lowered his voice. "These people—your parents and the volunteers and maybe some of the younger kids— they think climbing this wall is hard. They think it'll be a real accomplishment to make it all the way up. But you know different."

Rocco blinked. "I do?"

"Fighting cancer is harder than any wall. It's harder than freaking Mount Everest. But you're fighting it. And every day you're still here is a win for you. Compared to that, this wall is nothing."

Rocco looked away. "Is that the speech they tell you to give all the kids?"

"No. It's the speech I used to give myself, on the

days when I was puking up my guts or everything ached so much I wanted to cry, but I didn't have any tears left—on the days when I was sick to death of being sick to death."

Rocco's eyes met his, the hostility fading. "What are you talking about?"

Paul grabbed the hem of his shirt and jerked it up. "See that scar?" he asked.

The boy peered at the puckered line of flesh on Paul's chest. His eyes widened.

"Medication port. I bet you have one, too."

Rocco nodded. "You had cancer?"

"Leukemia. When I was your age. Three rounds of chemo. Radiation. Finally a bone-marrow transplant."

"They're talking about a transplant for me if this new chemo doesn't work." His eyes searched Paul's. The fear was still there, but something else crowded against it—the beginnings of hope. "And you're okay now?"

"One hundred percent. I climbed Denali—Mount McKinley—a little over a month ago."

Rocco swallowed, as if choking down strong emotion. "Wow."

"So are you gonna climb with me or not?"

Rocco glanced at the wall again, then back at Paul. "Yeah. Yeah, I'll climb with you."

"Great. Let's get you some gear."

No more running. The look in Rocco's eyes—that tiny glimmer of hope—hit Paul like a lightning bolt.

He'd been worried seeing these kids would bring back all the pain and despair of those months in the hospital, when all along he'd been missing his chance to let go of those memories and replace them with this joy.

This felt like summiting his first big mountain all over again. He wanted to shout and tell someone.

He wanted to tell Sierra.

The memory of her grinding her way up the trail on Uncompahgre sobered him. She'd accused him of running away from real life on the mountains. She'd had it right, almost. It wasn't life he was trying to escape up there, so much as memories of his past and fears of his future.

"I'm ready." Rocco, fitted with a helmet and climbing harness, turned to him.

"Me, too." Paul buckled his own helmet and clipped Rocco to the safety line. "Let's do this."

He wasn't a scared little boy with cancer anymore— he was a man who'd almost let the great gift he'd been given slip by him. By means of grace or a miracle or his own refusal to give up, he had a future, and he wasn't going to take that for granted ever again.

SIERRA REALIZED THAT dinner with Mark and Tabitha was a bad idea before the first course was delivered. Though the two lovebirds refrained from overt public displays of affection, they were so obviously in love— unable to keep their eyes off each other or their attention focused on anyone else for long—that Sierra felt she now knew what it was like to be invisible.

Maybe she should have accepted Mark's offer to fix her up with Tabitha's brother, but the thought of meeting anyone new left her cold.

She said an early good-night to the happy couple and hurried home to her apartment, where she switched on the computer and settled in to write. She was aware of the irony of the moment; she was using the same classic escape mechanism she'd accused Paul of, running away to work. He lost himself on a mountaintop, while she lost herself in the lines on her computer screen.

Currently she was working on a profile of a woman who had been inspired by the loss of a younger brother to cancer to pursue her medical degree. Dr. Felicity Alvarez had established a ground-breaking program for coordinating medical care for the city's poorest children—those who lived in housing projects and homeless shelters. Sierra had no doubt *Cherché*'s readers would find her story inspiring.

Writing about the brother who'd died, however, only made Sierra think of Paul. Even work was no longer the escape she'd hoped for—damn the man. Two thousand miles across the country and he was still messing up her life.

Impulsively, before she could chicken out or talk herself out of it, she grabbed her phone and punched in his number. Yes, she had done it so many times, she now had the ten digits memorized. She'd always hung up before he'd answered, but this time she let it ring.

And ring. On the sixth ring, a tinny rendition of his voice filled her ears. "Hey, it's Paul. Leave a message and I'll get back to you."

What could she say? *You're driving me crazy! I can't stop thinking about you?*

I think I love you?

She hung up and sat staring at the silent receiver. Yes, apparently it was possible to love a man she'd only known a week. Of course, they'd spent a great deal of time together during her time in Ouray—as much as some couples spent together in relationships that lasted months.

So maybe the length of their acquaintance didn't make such a big difference. There was the distance problem, but she was willing to compromise. She could move to Ouray. She liked it there. It reminded her of the little California town where she'd grown up. She could work from there.

She'd even be okay with some climbing if he'd stick to local fourteeners. But she didn't want him risking his life on major peaks. She didn't want to lose him.

But it wasn't only that. She wanted to know she mattered more than those damn mountains.

And that was the problem with him asking her to move in with him—it was too practical. He said he wanted to be with her, that he loved her even. But he might as well have been declaring he loved sunny days or cheese enchiladas. Where was the *passion?*

Her eyes burned and she blinked rapidly. She refused to cry over Paul. He wasn't worth the tears.

And he wasn't worth all this fretting. She turned resolutely back to the computer and began typing: *Felicity Alvarez took one of life's greatest losses and turned it into a victory, for herself and for the hundreds of children whose lives she has saved...*

PAUL DECIDED HE'D RATHER navigate Everest's icy crevasses than Manhattan during rush hour. And Sierra believed *mountains* were dangerous, he thought, narrowly avoiding being run down by a taxi as he darted across the street. He caused a minor traffic jam of his own as he paused on the sidewalk to stare up at the buildings that towered overhead, then the crowd of pedestrians adjusted and flowed around him. Which one of these buildings was his destination? It was like being stuck in a slot canyon, surrounded by towering cliff walls. Which route was the way out?

"You need directions, bud?" A gruff-looking man in a jacket with the name of a delivery service over the pocket stopped beside Paul.

"Uh, yeah. I'm looking for 250 West Fifty-Seventh."

"You're almost there." The man pointed. "That white building with the big planters on either side of the entrance."

"Thanks."

"No problem. Enjoy your stay in New York."

The man moved on. How had he known Paul was new to the city? Paul chuckled. Maybe the hiking boots and fully loaded backpack were his first clue.

He hoisted the pack a little higher on his shoulders and set off for the white building with the planters. Once inside, he studied the building directory.

"Sir? May I help you?" A granite-faced security guard approached.

"No, thanks. I know where I'm headed now." He turned toward the elevator.

The guard stepped in front of him. "Sir, where are you headed?"

"Eighth floor."

"Do you have an appointment?"

"No." He frowned. The whole point of this visit was to surprise Sierra.

"You can't go up without an appointment."

"I just need to go up for a minute to say hello to a friend."

"No one is allowed up without an appointment."

Paul understood the need for security, but this was maddening—not to mention the guard was spoiling his plan. "Call upstairs and ask for Mark Ekstein," he said. "He's an editor at *Great Outdoors*. Tell him Paul Teasdale is here to see him."

"Mr. Ekstein works on the tenth floor," the guard said. "You said you wanted the eighth floor."

"Just call him. Please."

Watching him as if he expected Paul to make a break for it at any second, the guard stepped behind a desk and picked up a black telephone handset. A few moments later he returned. "Mr. Ekstein is on his way down."

The guard continued to stare while Paul pretended to study the building directory once more. Several people gave him curious looks as they passed, all of them approaching the elevator unmolested. Maybe if Paul had worn a suit and carried a briefcase, the guard wouldn't have accosted him.

The elevator doors parted and a tall man with thinning dark hair stepped out. "Paul? What are you doing in Manhattan?"

Paul moved over, out of earshot of the guard, and explained his dilemma. "It's all right, Stewart," Mark said to the guard. "I'll take Mr. Teasdale up with me."

"He'll have to leave the backpack," the guard said.

Paul started to argue, then thought better of it. "Fine," he said, shrugging out of the pack. "But if anything happens to it, I'm holding you responsible."

He suppressed a grin as the guard struggled under the weight of the pack, then followed Mark into the elevator. "It's great to finally meet you," Mark said.

"You, too." He wanted to ask about Sierra—was she all right? Did she ever talk about him? Was she dating anyone else? But he'd know the answers to those questions soon enough, so he kept quiet.

"What did you want to see me about?" Mark asked as the elevator rose swiftly toward the fourteenth floor.

"I'm hoping you can get me in to see Sierra," Paul said. "The guard wouldn't let me go up by myself and I'm hoping to surprise her."

"Sierra? Sure, I can take you to her." Mark leaned forward and punched the button for eight. Paul waited for him to ask more questions, but Mark merely gave him a speculative look and remained silent.

The elevator stopped on the eighth floor and Mark led Paul through a pair of frosted-glass doors, past a receptionist Mark addressed as Stephanie and down a thickly carpeted hallway. The air smelled like floral perfume and fresh-brewed coffee, and as they passed open office doors Paul heard snippets of conversations, the whir of printers and faxes, and ringing telephones. Mark stopped at a door near the end of the hall. "Sierra, there's someone here to see you."

Paul had spent a lot of time these past weeks thinking about her, but his memories didn't do her justice. He had to remind himself to breathe as he stared at her. She was even more beautiful than he remembered, but also more polished. She wore her hair swept back from her face with combs. Dressed in a trim black suit, purple blouse and purple heels with bows at the ankles, everything about her screamed city sophistication. Paul was conscious of his own wrinkled hiking pants and T-shirt. No wonder the guard had looked at him as if he was someone from another planet.

"Paul?" She stared at him, her expression some-where between delight and distress. "What are you doing here?"

"I'm doing some fundraising and publicity for a new project I'm working on."

Which wasn't at all what he'd meant to say. *I came to see you,* were the proper words—the true ones. But when he'd opened his mouth that other safe, practical speech came out. It was true, too, but not the truth that concerned her. "I wanted to see you," he added, he hoped not too late.

"I'll leave you two alone now," Mark said, and slipped away. Paul wondered if Sierra even noticed. Her eyes remained fixed on him.

"What kind of project?" she asked.

He sat in the chair across from her, hoping she'd sit also, but she remained standing. "I'm starting up a camp for critically ill children," he said. "A place where they can come and spend time in the mountains, away from their illness, but still receive the care they need." After working with Rocco that day at the pool, he'd discovered there was no permanent place in that part of Colorado for children and their families to visit, only occasional pieced-together trips. His camp would be able to serve many more children from hos-pitals all over the United States.

"You are? That's great, that'll be a good project for you between climbs."

"No more climbs," he said. "Well, maybe a fourteener here and there, but I'm hanging up my gear. Running my camp is going to be a full-time job."

Another one of those looks he couldn't read. If he hadn't known better, he'd have thought she was about to cry. "What brought this on?" she asked.

"A lot of things. Meeting you, for one." She had said he'd have to quit climbing in order for them to be together. At the time, it had seemed like too much of a sacrifice, but a lot of things had changed since then. "I realized there's more to life than bagging the next peak," he said. "I thought climbing made me feel more alive, but I realize now that I can get a bigger rush—a bigger affirmation that life is worth living—by helping kids get out in nature and discover all they're capable of."

"That's wonderful."

You're wonderful. But what if she didn't feel the same about him anymore? He'd gone over this meeting in his head a thousand times on the flight over. Everything went perfectly in his mind, but now that he was here, the possibility of rejection paralyzed him. He cleared his throat, trying to keep the conversation going while he worked up his courage. He wasn't normally a coward, but this moment mattered so much— more than anything he'd ever done. "I was able to use my reputation and my contacts to line up sponsors and donors for the new camp," he said. "I've got some land not far from Ouray and we've already started construction on cabins and a main lodge and clinic. We're hoping to open next summer."

"Oh. That's great." She lowered herself into the chair behind her desk.

None of this was going the way he'd planned. She was supposed to rush into his arms and declare how much she'd missed him. He groped for something else to say, to shift the mood to something more upbeat. His gaze settled on her purse, resting on the corner of her desk. "I see you still have the netsuke." He nodded to the red dragon that hung from the bag.

"Oh, yes. Thank you again for sending it. It means a lot."

"I never should have kept it. I know Victor would have wanted you to have it."

"I don't think he'd have minded you keeping it for a while. I think my father would have liked you."

Great, but what did *she* think of him? "I was hoping you could help me," he said.

"Help you? Does Mark want me to write an article about your camp?" She glanced toward the doorway, which the editor had long since vacated.

"No. I was hoping…" He took a deep breath, then rushed on. "I was hoping you'd agree to help with the camp. I need someone to handle publicity and work with the media. It doesn't pay much, but it comes with a cabin and…and we'd be near each other."

"You're offering me a job?"

He winced. This was going worse than that trip to Disney when he was a kid. He needed to fix this. "A job if you want it. And a place to live. I…I want us to be together and I thought this was a way to do it, without rushing you into anything."

"Of course not. We wouldn't want to rush." Her voice held a chill that was reflected in her eyes. His stomach hurt.

"What do you think?" he asked.

"I think your camp sounds great. And I'm glad you're not climbing anymore."

"I mean, what do you think about my offer?"

She avoided his eyes, her gaze focused on the papers on her desk. "It was good of you to think of me, but I'll have to pass."

He gripped the arms of the chair until his knuckles ached. "You're sure you won't reconsider?"

"No. It was great to see you, and I appreciate the offer, but I really do have a lot of work to do."

He might have been a salesman she was trying to get rid of. So much for thinking she loved him the way he loved her. How could he have misread her so badly? He stood. "I guess I'll be going then."

"Have a nice time in New York."

The same words had been spoken to him moments before by a stranger. He and Sierra might have been strangers, for all the coldness between them now. He turned and stalked out of the office before he made an even bigger fool of himself.

SIERRA PUT HER HANDS flat on her desk, steadying herself and breathing deeply. For a moment, when Paul had appeared in her doorway, she'd been full of hope. She'd waited for him to declare his love for her—to say he couldn't live without her and wanted to be with her forever.

Instead he'd offered her a job! What a fool she'd been.

She stared at the netsuke, the dragon leering at her mockingly. Ripping it from her purse, she went to hurl it across the room, but ended up clutching it in her hand, the carved jade digging into her skin, a mere pricking compared to the pain that flooded her chest. She put her head down on her desk and closed her eyes, wishing she could erase the past ten minutes.

"Dammit, I'm not going to let things end this way!"

The shout reverberated through the office. Sierra raised her head and stared at Paul, who had reappeared in her office doorway.

But this was a man transformed. His eyes blazed, his whole body tensed with emotion. She stared. "Paul, what are you doing?" she asked.

"What I meant to do before." He crossed the room in three strides and pulled her out of her chair. "Sierra, I love you and I want to be with you. You wouldn't live with me before when you knew I'd leave you to climb, but I promise, I won't do that. My feelings for you haven't changed and they aren't going to."

"I…I've never seen you like this," she stammered. So emotional. So *passionate*.

"What do you want from me? Do you want me to

get down on my knees? I will." He dropped to one knee in front of her. "Sierra, marry me."

"Marry you?"

"I won't leave until you say yes."

"Yes."

He stood, his face paler, though his eyes still blazed. "Yes, you'll marry me?"

"Yes!" The word had just popped out when he'd made his incredible offer, but she realized she'd never meant anything more. "I thought you came here to offer me a job," she said.

"The job's still yours," he said. "Though no more private cabin. You'll have to live with me."

"That was your idea of a romantic offer—a job and a cabin?" She suddenly felt like laughing.

He looked almost sheepish. "I scared you off before, asking you to move in with me," he said. "I wasn't going to make that mistake again."

"You goof!" She punched his chest. "All I wanted was to know you really cared."

"I do care, Sierra. I love you."

"More than you love mountains?" She already knew the answer, but she wanted to hear him say it.

"More than mountains. More than anything."

"And I love you. I think I've loved you since that first day I saw you up on that roof, but I've been too afraid to admit it." Her vision blurred, eyes stinging.

"You won't mind leaving Manhattan?"

"I can always come back and visit." She sniffed and

wiped at her eyes. "The truth is, I missed Ouray—and not just because you were there. I missed the mountains. I guess I'm my father's daughter after all."

"Are you crying?" He touched her cheek. "You never cry."

He was right. She never cried. But these were definitely tears flowing down her face now—happy ones. "And you never get angry, but you were angry just now."

"I was angry at myself for being such an idiot. I'm used to taking risks in the mountains, but when it comes to real life, I guess I've been playing it too safe."

"I'm glad you took another chance with me."

"We'll start over together," he said. "We'll make a great team."

"Can we do it?" she asked. "Is love really enough?"

"It's enough," he said.

"I believe you." Love was enough to make her change her whole life, and she wasn't the only one. She and Paul could build something together, and they'd help each other over the rough spots. All the risks would be worth it to be together.

* * * * *

HARLEQUIN® Super Romance®

COMING NEXT MONTH

Available June 29, 2010

HARLEQUIN®

A Romance

FOR EVERY MOOD™

Spotlight on
— Heart & Home —

Heartwarming romances
where love can happen
right when you least expect it.

See the next page to enjoy a sneak peek
from Silhouette Special Edition®,
a Heart and Home series.

*Introducing McFARLANE'S PERFECT BRIDE
by* USA TODAY *bestselling author Christine Rimmer,
from Silhouette Special Edition®.*

Entranced. Captivated. Enchanted.

Connor sat across the table from Tori Jones and couldn't help thinking that those words exactly described what effect the small-town schoolteacher had on him. He might as well stop trying to tell himself he wasn't interested. He was powerfully drawn to her.

Clearly, he should have dated more when he was younger.

There had been a couple of other women since Jennifer had walked out on him. But he had never been entranced. Or captivated. Or enchanted.

Until now.

He wanted her—*her*, Tori Jones, in particular. Not just someone suitably attractive and well-bred, as Jennifer had been. Not just someone sophisticated, sexually exciting and discreet, which pretty much described the two women he'd dated after his marriage crashed and burned.

It came to him that he...he *liked* this woman. And that was new to him. He liked her quick wit, her wisdom and her big heart. He liked the passion in her voice when she talked about things she believed in.

He liked *her.* And suddenly it mattered all out of proportion that she might like him, too.

Was he losing it? He couldn't help but wonder. Was he cracking under the strain—of the soured economy, the McFarlane House setbacks, his divorce, the scary changes in his son? Of the changes he'd decided he needed to make in his life and himself?

Strangely, right then, on his first date with Tori Jones, he didn't care if he just might be going over the edge. He was having a great time—having *fun*, of all things—and he didn't want it to end.

Is Connor finally able to admit his feelings to Tori, and are they reciprocated?
Find out in McFARLANE'S PERFECT BRIDE
by USA TODAY bestselling author Christine Rimmer.
Available July 2010,
only from Silhouette Special Edition®.

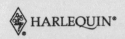